Such Waltzing Was Not Easy

ILLINOIS SHORT FICTION

SUCH WALTZING WAS NOT EASY

Stories by
GORDON WEAVER

UNIVERSITY OF ILLINOIS PRESS

Urbana   Chicago   London

The following stories appeared originally, in somewhat different form, as follows:

"When Times Sit In," *Perspective*, vol. XIII, no. 1, 1962

"Wave the Old Wave," *Epoch*, vol. XIII, no. 2, Winter, 1964

"Low Blue Man," *North American Review*, vol. 250, no. 1, Spring, 1965

"The Day I Lost My Distance," *Minnesota Review*, vol. VI, no. 1, 1966

"Kiss in the Hand," *US Catholic*, vol. XXXII, no. 10, February, 1967

"Gold Moments and Victory Beer," *December*, vol. XI, nos. 2 & 3, 1967

"I Go Back," *US Catholic*, vol. XXXIV, no. 3, July, 1968

"Cemetery in Winter," *Latitudes*, vol. II, no. 4, Spring, 1972

"The Two Sides of Things," *North American Review*, vol. 258, no. 2, Summer, 1973

"Granger Hunting," *The Southern Review*, vol. X, no. 3, Summer, 1974

Library of Congress Cataloging in Publication Data

Weaver, Gordon.
    Such waltzing was not easy.

    (Illinois short fiction)
    CONTENTS: The day I lost my distance.—Low blue man.
—Granger hunting. [etc.]
    I. Title.
PZ4.W3628Su   [PS3573.E17]   813'.5'4   75-2288
ISBN 0-252-00476-0
ISBN 0-252-00533-3 pbk.

*for Nelson, Rosemary, David, and Donald . . .
and, always, for Judy, Kris, and Anna*

Contents

The whiskey on your breath
Could make a small boy dizzy;
But I hung on like death:
Such waltzing was not easy.

—Theodore Roethke,
from "My Papa's Waltz"

The Day I Lost My Distance

My sister Jane thought I was a stupid boy and a coward, too—until the day I lost my distance. I began with it each morning. I began with it the day I lost it.

We had a broken home. My parents were divorced when I was nine, in 1945, and my mother and I lived with my sister through most of the last year of the war.

I shared a small bedroom in the old house with my nephew and niece, Jane's children. At exactly 6:17 each morning, as I dressed for school, the house trembled and the dirt-speckled pane in the bedroom's only window rattled at the passing of a freight train; we lived three doors away from the south side tracks of the Milwaukee Road. My nephew and niece slept while I pulled on my underwear, socks, trousers, and polo shirt. It was April, and the mornings were chilly, the sky outside gray with industrial haze. I swallowed a delicious desire to shiver.

The bedroom was halfway below the level of the cement walk that ran beside the house, leading me to the street where I went, to see, each morning before breakfast, before anyone else was out of bed. Through the window I could see only the next house—where the lawless Lenski boys lived—about six feet away. One morning I saw a large gray rat walk ponderously past the window, as if he had gorged all night on the pigeons in one of the lofts maintained by the neighborhood's older boys.

I must have overslept this morning—a Monday—for the train did not pass, the house did not shake gently on its foundation. I hurried, but it was too late. I heard my sister Jane running the tap at the kitchen sink until the water came cold for the coffee pot. She often said she could not face the morning without fresh coffee. I braced, calling upon my talent for distance, and went into the kitchen.

"Well, good morning," Jane said, and stared at me. She didn't have her glasses on yet, so had to tilt her head back and focus on me from beneath the rims of her lowered eyelids. Her face was pale, puffed with sleep, her hair smudged out of order by her pillow. "Where are you going, Oskar?" I pretended to scrub the gummy traces of sleep from my eyes with my thumbs as an excuse for not answering her.

Jane didn't seem to care. An event the day before had pretty much decided her; I wasn't worth the trouble. She turned away to scratch a kitchen match on the blackened stove grating. She held it at the edge of the front stove burner, the gas popped, and she slid the coffee pot over the flame. I knew that she was planning on a ten-minute half-sleep while the water boiled, so I hoped to be free to go outside in a moment.

"Are you looking for trouble?" she said. "You better stay inside or that Menke snot'll clout you again." She was taunting me—and why not? She thought I deserved it.

"I can't help it," I said, but she was not interested in any excuse. She took a cigarette from the package in her bathrobe pocket, bent over to light it at the small lick of blue-yellow flame that curled up around the bottom of the heavy-breathing coffee pot.

"You could for Christ's sake try slapping him back," she said wearily, without the bitterness she could usually muster. Cigarette smoke came out of her mouth as she spoke; she coughed, blew out the rest of the smoke, and—yanking the knot in her bathrobe cord tighter—she walked back to her bedroom, her bare feet whispering on the kitchen-floor linoleum. My mother was still sleeping on the couch in the living room when I went out the back door to use what time I had left before breakfast. I wasn't worried about Kenny Menke, the boy who had slapped me on Sunday; there was never anyone else outside that early.

We played war on Sunday, as we played it every day. I slept late on

Sundays, for none of the other boys would be ready to play until they had returned from Mass at the Cathedral on the other side of the railroad tracks. We were the only non-Catholic family in the neighborhood; my mother had given up church during the war. Organized religion merited none of her attention; it had not stopped the government from drafting my older brothers, Milt and Len, nor had it prevented the end of her marriage after twenty-five years.

By the time I got up on Sunday, my sister was drinking coffee and reading the newspaper at the kitchen table; my mother was drinking coffee and watching my sister, waiting for a chance to begin talking about their jobs, the Polish neighbors, or the last V-mail from one of my brothers—and my niece and nephew were outside, playing.

We had an unusually large game of war that Sunday and I thought it had started very well, for I was one of the Americans. Kenny Menke was our commander because he was eleven and the biggest. We were about to embark on some sort of spying mission.

It was a privilege for me to be an American in the war for a change. Ever since my brother Milt had sent me a German steel helmet as a souvenir of Belgium (he had taken part in the Battle of the Bulge), I had been a German, forced to suffer defeat each day, for our Germans always lost.

Generally we Germans sat in a huge, natural foxhole in a vacant corner lot, huddling next to the dirt parapet, awaiting the commando charge of Kenny Menke and his fellow Americans. They came screaming across the no-man's-land of the lot, firing their weapons at us, jumping into our foxhole—there were never more than three or four of us, the youngest, most timid in the neighborhood—shooting us at close range, impaling us on bayonets of the imagination, pummeling us half-hard with fists, finally taking us prisoner, tying us with ropes, after which they raised the flag and Kenny Menke made a speech about victory.

Through it all, I remained at a distance. I glowered from under the rim of my precious German helmet at the advancing Americans, sometimes imagining how I could pick off Kenny Menke as he led the enemy toward me. Sometimes I tried to imagine the emotions of the surely dead German who must have worn my helmet and watched his enemies approach him with death in their hands.

When the Americans leaped into our foxhole, I never shouted "We surrender!" and never raised my hands, like my comrades. I withdrew, inwardly, to watch myself being spitted by Kenny Menke, to imagine the exotic qualities of death and defeat—and the pummeling my captors gave me never hurt quite so much, for I was not there, not *with* them. . . . I was merely a consciousness, somehow mixed with the ghostly consciousness of an unknown German soldier who had expired in just such a way in a hedgerow somewhere in Belgium. So I did not mind losing, dying each day in the game of war; not too much, anyway.

This Sunday I was an American. The novelty of it made me bold. Kenny Menke held a short briefing behind the hulk of an old Terraplane auto that had once belonged to the Lenski boys. They had run it around the neighborhood, using naphtha for fuel, until the mother of some smaller children had complained to the police and the police had caught them and driven them home in a squad car. The Lenski boys had had no driver's licenses.

Kenny Menke was wearing a new gas-mask carrier slung over one shoulder. Since he was our commander, he wore not a helmet, but an Army Air Corps officer's hat with a fifty-mission crush in it. I think he carried a cast-iron toy Luger and wore a webbed belt with a canteen on it. Also, puttees.

I had never seen the gas-mask carrier, so it jarred my sense of order. War had an order for me, and I spoke rather than see order violated wantonly.

"Commando leaders don't carry gas masks," I said.

"Don't carry gas masks?" he snarled. "Whad'ya think they use for gas, dopus?"

"The first thing they throw away is their gas masks," I said. I had been told that by my oldest brother, Nils, a 4-F who lived and worked in Davenport, Iowa. It was a mistake to say it. Kenny Menke couldn't tolerate rebellion in his ranks—he was too stupid to care if I was right or not—and I might just as well have accommodated his gas-mask carrier with an alteration in my vision of the order of war. Also, his brother Warren, thirteen, was with us. He was a tyrant, a cut below the lawless Lenski boys and a boy named Adamowski, who could whip everyone—so he came to check on us groundlings often.

"The Secret Service uses 'em," Warren said. He lied of course.

"The Secret Service uses 'em dopus!" Kenny spat in my face. Now I was the center of attention—and I realized how foolhardy I had been. Still, I spoke.

"That's baloney," I said. "They throw them away the first chance they get, because no one uses gas any more." Kenny Menke stood with his mouth open, not at all sure what he ought to do; he lacked the brains to realize that he could silence me by simply denying it loudly. But his brother Warren was older, a shade more vicious.

"He's calling you a liar, Kenny," he said. This Kenny could understand. He took one giant step up to me, set his feet firmly, twisted his trunk, and slapped me across the face. My face went red and hot, my eyes watered, and the German helmet slipped down, blinding me. Kenny Menke readied his arm to hit me again, his brother Warren snickered vindictively, and the other Americans hollered across no-man's-land to the Germans to hurry up and come, there was going to be a fight.

But I knew there wasn't going to be one, and there wasn't. I reached up with my free hand—I carried a wooden model of a Springfield .03 rifle—and tilted my helmet far enough back so that I could see dimly through the film of tears that stung my eyes, and I walked away. Behind me I was called names, whistled at, challenged by some smaller boys, rechallenged by Kenny Menke, but this didn't hurt. Already I was away from them, examining and re-experiencing what had happened to me, sorting out the thoughts and feelings that were going through me—and through the others.

By the time I had reached my sister's house, my slapped face had subsided to a warm glow in my cheek, and I was safe . . . at a distance. I went into our back yard, ignored my niece and nephew, and sat on the wooden steps in the rear of the yard, looking across the alley at the rear of the tannery. Yes, we lived at the rear of the tannery. I watched the piles of hides and the bins of salt as I put myself into a kind of rhythm with the dormant tone of the idle Sunday appearance of the tannery yard.

"Play with us, Oskar. Come on and wrestle or something," my nephew said to me.

"Go away," I told him, and he did. He went in and told his mother that I was outside, crying. Jane called to me from the back door, and I had to go in and explain.

"Goddamn those Polacks," my sister said.

"Kenny Menke's not Polish," I said.

"For God's sake, what are *you* standing up for him for!" Jane said. My mother said nothing; she only took a washcloth and wiped my streaked face.

"I'm not asking you to like living around a bunch of damn snot Polacks," Jane said, "but you can't seem to find enough pride to defend yourself. Do you want to grow up letting people like that wipe their feet on you? Your mother's not raising you to be a doormat for Polacks, Oskar."

"Leave him alone, Jane," my mother said finally. "He feels bad enough."

"I'm all right," I said. And I was. Except that I nagged myself for having brought Kenny Menke's slap on with my own foolish tongue, my foolish insistence, my failure to remember that things—even Kenny Menke's ignorance and stupidity—were best enjoyed at a distance. Nothing he or anyone could do, I thought, could disturb the order and balance I could impose on things if only I remembered to keep from touching them.

"What should he do?" Jane asked. "Go around acting like he's no better than they are? If he doesn't learn to stand up to them, then he won't be as *good* as they are. You won't be as good as a damn Polack!" Jane told me.

"Just remember, Oskar," my mother said, perhaps to mollify Jane, "that you're no foundry worker's boy, and you're no railroad brakeman's boy. You're better than that."

"I'm not going to see him grow up like them," Jane promised.

My sister was very bitter. Her husband was in the navy, stationed in Florida, guarding Japanese prisoners of war. She did not like her job in the county courthouse steno pool, and there was not enough money for her to move from the neighborhood. She had no delusions or false pride, but she knew that it was not right for her to have to put her children in a day nursery, and it was not right for her to have to live next to a tannery and a railroad in the midst of hard-drinking factory workers who spoke Polish and bred swarms of dirty children who grew from a state of neglected, grimy childhood to an adolescence of banditry, like the Lenski boys. She was afraid. Her children might become like those around them; I might—in time; perhaps she feared she might. I think that only I was unafraid.

Until this day, this Monday. Once I was outside, there was too much to see for me to care about what had happened the day before. I had to watch the sun break and then slowly dissolve the industrial haze that hung over the fires of the foundry cupolas in the distance behind the tannery. I had to see the sameness of things, the order. I had to *know* the order. The haze broke, and there was morning.

The order began. First there was the tannery; workers on the day shift arrived, flipped and stacked the hides on castered platforms with the aid of sharp hooks that gleamed in curves from their fists, swearing in Polish as they unlocked bins and shoveled salt into barrels, the smell of the activated tanning vats rising on the wind like a signal. Next there was the front of the house: two service-star flags in our front windows to represent my brothers who were on two opposite sides of the world from me; the second-floor windows hiding Mrs. Lewandowski, who drank and had passed out in a snowbank at Christmas and so lost all the toes on her feet to the cold and might never walk again; and her husband Adrian, the railroad brakeman, who also drank but had never been frozen yet. Then the street: to the left lived the Lenskis, who might be plotting a crime; directly across the street, the house with a small barn where an older boy lived—he smoked cigarettes and kept pigeons, which the rats ate with regularity. Next to the barn was the house where Donnie Repka lived.

He was only four or five and, like me, had no friends. Even adults avoided him, and to my sister Jane he symbolized the malevolence of the neighborhood in his small body. He never appeared during the winter, but as soon as the snow melted, his mother locked him out of the house from early morning to dinner time. He wore no shoes or underwear, nothing but faded bib overalls.

He had a way of lying in wait at the corner of his house. Anyone who passed in front of his house on the sidewalk was fair game. My sister knew this, but she would not walk home in the evening on the other side of the street. She got off the streetcar that had brought her to the neighborhood from downtown, and she marched past Donnie Repka's, holding her shoulders stiffly, poised to run. I had seen it many times.

Donnie waited until she was directly in front of his house, and then he charged. He ran clumsily, with his legs spread wide, holding himself at his open fly with both his dirty hands, screaming in a mad glee, "I'll pee on you, I'll pee on you!"

Jane gave herself one split second in which to stop and focus all her hatred on him with her large eyes, and then she raised her skirts above her knees and began to run. "The *hell* you will!" she shouted back over her shoulder at him, lengthening her stride to outdistance him. He would not go beyond the border of his front yard, and he never caught her. I always had to hide before Jane got to our house so she would not see me laughing.

Next to Donnie Repka's lived Adamowski, the strongest boy in the neighborhood. He was only fifteen, but even the Lenski boys left him alone. He took the military insignia, which we all collected, away from us whenever he found something he liked. He twisted the arms of the safety cadets at school, refused the orders of teachers, swore whenever he wished, had been chased by a policeman.

To the right of my sister's house, on our side of the street, lived Virgie Barczak. My sister disliked her intensely, too. Her father worked for the railroad, but in an office, so her mother never spoke to her neighbors or the neighborhood children. Virgie was unpopular because she dressed well and went to a Catholic parochial school. On Sundays, when the Barczaks had returned from Mass, Virgie didn't change to everyday clothes, but promenaded on the walk in front of her house, swinging a purse, sneering at the boys who played war on the lot and at the girls who skipped rope and played hopscotch and jacks and wrote boys' names on the sidewalk with chalk. Once I found Virgie's elaborate rosary on the walk, where she must have dropped it in the course of her promenade. I showed it to my sister Jane, who made me put it back where I had found it. She wouldn't allow me to give it back to its owner personally.

"Shouldn't he give it back to the little girl, Jane?" my mother said.

"If they think so much of their beads, let them take better care of them or else go out and find them on the street themselves," Jane said. She would not have me running any errands for Polish Catholics.

Then there was the railroad. I did not actually go any nearer to the tracks than Virgie's house, not after the unknown man's death. Before he was killed, I used to climb the bank and stand on the ties to look both ways for the next train. I put my ear against the rails to hear its approach, and there was always the same steady electric hum. When a train was passing, I retreated down the bank and spied, secretly, on the men in the engine cab as it passed, seeing them, but not being seen—apart from them, but knowing and seeing, fitting them into my ordered reality.

One Saturday night a Polish wedding was held on the other side of the tracks. It must have been quite an affair, for the unknown man did not start for home until just before daylight. He had undoubtedly been very drunk and could not have felt the wheels of the train pass over him. Perhaps he had gone to sleep on the tracks.

The other children were still at Mass when I went to see the railroad. The first thing I saw was a finger—the unknown man's finger, nothing more. His limbs were scattered, and the bulk of him, unrecognizable, was like the bodies of cats I had seen crushed flat in the streets. I couldn't escape from that. Blood, bones, and flesh were real, and yet the wreckage I saw was not a man, not a thing to be seen and understood and called *a man*. My distance did not serve me.

My screaming brought people outside, and soon other boys, back from Mass, came running to see the man. Jane came out and took me into the house. Even Donnie Repka left his front yard and, finding the unknown man's arm with his wristwatch intact and the expansion band unbroken, he slipped it over the stump and ran home with it. When a policeman came to get the watch, Donnie howled terribly and urinated on the policeman's leg. His mother had to throw water on him.

So the railroad was to be seen only from the distance of Virgie Barczak's front walk. It was a dangerous thing, capable at one stroke of making death very real; I didn't dare to go very close. I could still stand and watch and read the names of the great companies painted on the boxcars, but it was several days before I could put the sight of the unknown man into its rightful place in my pattern.

This Monday morning, as usual, the time for me to go in to breakfast was announced by the seven o'clock bells at the Cathedral and by the emergence of the older boy across the street, who came outside wearing slippers, clearing his throat, spitting, smoking a first cigarette, like an adult. I watched him enter his barn, then emerge again in his pigeon loft, where he released the pigeons—and they flew out, uncertainly silhouetted against the gold haze of sky behind them.

My sister was having coffee and a cigarette at the kitchen table. She held my nephew between her knees while she combed his hair with wave set. He didn't like it because it made his hair hard as a rock, but she was determined that he would not look unkept like the other children at the day nursery. My mother, who took her grandchildren to the nursery on her way to work and picked them up in the evening, had jelly toast ready for me.

"I have to eat in a hurry today and get to school early," I said. My mother found my school books and set them on the table beside me.

"Why?" Jane asked me.

"Because I don't want to meet Kenny Menke on the way to school and get in any more trouble."

"Jesus wept!" Jane said.

"You've had everything and you've had nothing," my mother said. She was talking about the divorce, about my father and the displacement of our family that had happened with the war. My nephew began to cry because Jane had pulled his hair too hard with the comb.

School that day was uneventful. I came home, ate some toast, looked at a comic book I had already read twice, and because my mother and my sister would not return for at least half an hour, I took my German helmet and my .03 rifle and went to the lot to play war. I didn't think it was odd that Kenny Menke made me a German again. I didn't care. It happened very quickly.

The Americans charged us, firing, throwing grenades, yelling, and I say Kenny Menke leading them. It was a discovery, like my discovery of the unknown man on the railroad tracks. I knew that he intended to use the excuse of the assault to do a better job of what he had started the day before. Contrary to the rules of war, I climbed out of our foxhole and began to run. The oversized helmet slipped down over my eyes, and I was blind, stumbling, not sure of my direction. All I wanted was to get away.

He caught me easily and hit me in the middle of the back with his fist. Because of my momentum and the unsureness of my footing, the blow made me pitch forward, the rim of the helmet bit into the back of my neck as I landed, and my palms and knees were painfully skinned. I said it without thinking.

"*Dupa!*" I said, rolling over and getting to my feet. Ass. *Dupa* is Polish for "ass." I never swore, not in Polish, though I knew all the words from watching and listening to the men at the tannery, nor in English. We all knew how to swear, but I did *not* swear. And it had happened without my thinking of it, without my wanting to—as if someone Polish had gotten inside me, spoken for me. I was not so much frightened of what he would do to me for cursing him as I was furious at myself for bringing it on with a word off my own tongue. My distance had failed me. I had failed it—betrayed myself. But Kenny Menke only stood bear-like, his mouth open; perhaps he had not even heard it.

"Did you hear what he called you?" Warren Menke said. Suddenly he was there to prod his brother. His eyes glittered with eagerness. The entire German and American armies were there, all to see the fight. "You let him do that? Kick his ass for him."

Kenny Menke stepped up to me and slapped my face again. "Take off the helmet," his brother said, smiling, "so's it's a fair fight." I took off the precious souvenir, and the last of my distance evaporated as I conceived a vision of the German soldier who must have worn it and known a moment like mine, when things were closing on him and the end of his life had come, one way or another.

I didn't know how to fight; I had to imitate Kenny, putting up my fists and circling. The German and American armies closed in a tighter ring and began to shout. I'm sure they all cheered for him, for he was a sure winner. We circled, and Kenny punched at me. He hit me on the forehead, and I could feel the spot swell to a stony lump. He hit me in the ear, and I felt it flame and redden. He was clumsy and a bit slower than I, and it seemed the fight would last forever. His brother became bored.

"Quit screwing around, Kenny," he said. "Like this!" He jumped on me, circled my neck with his arm, and squeezed. I could feel him straining and heard the muscles in my neck wrench, my ears ring, redness in front of my eyes. Then Jane came.

"Goddamnit!" she said. "Goddamn you!" Warren Menke had let go of me. I looked, choking, and saw my sister hit him again, expertly, as a girl who grew up with brothers would know how to hit— Warren Menke cried. I thought she had come to rescue me.

But she grabbed my shoulders, shook me, and turned me to face Kenny Menke, who stood immobile in shock. "*Now fight him, Oskar! Damn it, fight him!*" Jane said, and she pushed me toward him.

The noise was greater now. Everyone was there to see the fight. The Lenski boys whooped and cheered . . . for me. "Go it, you kid nothing!" they yelled. "Mix it, mix it," the boy with pigeons said around the cigarette between his lips. "Let's see you tangle assholes," Adamowski said professionally. Not just the boys and my sister, though, but girls my age, older, and adults. Railroad and foundry workers, mothers—all yelling, cheering, some in Polish, their mouths open, their teeth and tongues showing, all thrusting me toward the intimacy of fists with Kenny Menke. There was no way out.

They began to fill me. They filled me with the oppression that weighted them, with the burden of their disappointments, with the emptiness of their pleasure, with the thick sense of the eternal futility and insufficient grasp that they only half knew themselves. And powered by it, by them, I bore down on Kenny Menke.

Before he recovered himself, I had hit him squarely in the nose— "Hey-hey! Right in the snotlocker!" Adamowski yelled—and Kenny began to bleed. His blood ribboned down over his mouth, clogging his breathing, and each time he reached up with his guard to wipe it away, I stepped in and hit him again. He began to whine and grunt, then to cry silently, then to bawl and scream—and still I hit him. His eyes closed up, and I could stand openly in front of him and sink my fists in his stomach and, when he turned, thump him in the back of the head, in the kidneys, until finally he fell and didn't get up, and my sister took my hand and led me away—he was unrecognizable to me, yet I would have continued to hit him.

There was one long cheer as I left, as if they marked my beginning as a fighter, or my end—some kind of end of me. The crowd broke and went home, chuckling and conversing as though they had won a short rebellion against a master and were content now to return cheerfully to their cages. And they *had* won.

My sister wiped my face with her handkerchief, said she would put ice on the bump on my forehead. She led me home, holding my hand, stopping every so often to wipe her eyes, for she cried harder than I.

"Damn them, that'll show them," she said. "Damn them, we showed them." She didn't see, as I did, that they had beaten us— beaten me. My sister and the Polish people had beaten me. I was the loser. We were too excited and forgot where we were walking; we walked right past Donnie Repka's house. He charged, his eyes lit with opportunity.

"I'll pee on you, I'll pee on you all!" he hollered, running, opening his fly.

"Run, Oskar," Jane said, letting go of my hand. "Run for it," she said, already ahead of me.

"I'll pee on *you!*" Donnie said, bracing himself at the edge of his lawn. I carried my German helmet by the chin strap. I swiped wildly at him with it, and he ducked but lost his balance, fell on the grass, howling.

I started to run. I've been running from them ever since.

Low Blue Man

Just before Labor Day, when it was almost time for Franklin to be starting back to school again, mother told him that father would soon be paying him another visit. He was sitting in the sun parlor, reading a book, when mother told him.

"Your father's coming to see you tomorrow," mother said, wiping her wet hands on the dish towel. Franklin forgot all about the book. He looked at mother and said: "It's not my birthday again until next year, and Christmas comes before that."

Mother set her jaw in a way Franklin recognized, and looked at him for what seemed a long time before speaking. Something about father always did that to her. Sometimes mother would have waited long enough before speaking, but sometimes, too, she didn't wait long enough, and so said things she didn't like Franklin to hear.

"Maybe he wants to make his big splash while he's still got something left to do it with," mother said. Franklin saw that she was immediately sorry. As she did always at these times, she turned away from Franklin and went into the kitchen to be alone; he heard her snap the dish towel loudly before folding it to hang up.

He understood *big splash*. What mother meant by *big splash* was like the time of brother Bob's marriage. Father had come to make a big splash then, and Franklin had been the only one to see it besides brother Bob and father himself. Brother Bob was in the sun parlor, showing father his new spinning reel, and Franklin had come silently to the kitchen doorway, where he'd been looking at an avocado he was growing in a glass of water, and he'd seen and heard it all.

Father said, "Bobby, boy I had to get you something for your wedding, kid, and damned if I knew what, so I finally figured you could use a good pen." Father dipped his hand into his shirt pocket and gave brother Bob a brand new Parker 51 fountain pen with a gold cap and his name stamped on the barrel in gold.

Brother Bob smiled a little and kind of moved his shoulders, and said something like, "Dad . . . Hell, Dad . . . ," turning the fountain pen over and over in his hands, looking down at it and squinting, and then looking up at father and smiling and shrugging. And at just the moment when Franklin was going to shout out loud that *he* knew father was fooling, just then, father laughed his big laugh and cracked brother one on the arm.

"I got you a little scratch paper too, boy," he said, handing a little brown book to brother. Brother Bob looked in the book, and smiled some more, blinking.

"Well, I don't know what to say, Dad!" he said. Father laughed again, and cracked brother another good one, and then they shook hands like two people who loved each other.

Brother Dick came in from the front room just then, wearing his letter sweater from college, which he always wore when father came to visit, and he shouted, "Hi, Pete! Did you just get in?" to father, and father shook hands with him, and then Bob showed Franklin and brother Dick the bank account book with five hundred dollars in it that father had given him.

"Say," father said to brother Dick, "did I tell you I'm turning you pro now?" Then he explained to them all how he would pay brother Dick one dollar for every point he made next basketball season, and Dick should just send him the box scores from the newspaper, and he'd send a check right along—if brother Dick didn't have anything against New York banks, that is. They all laughed hard some more, and father got out a little bottle of something special a New York friend had brought from Canada for him, and he made three drinks, explaining that water only ruined it.

"Now, my littlest guy," he said to Franklin, "you take this and just hike yourself to the drugstore and get a soda or some peanuts or something you like," patting Franklin on the hinder and heading him toward the front-hall door. As he went out, Franklin heard father say, "He's the littlest dickens," and he and Bob and Dick laughed again. He didn't look at his hand until he was out of the house. Franklin was terribly surprised to find it was *five* dollars, not just one.

That was how father made a big splash. Perhaps he was coming this time to make up for not coming for Franklin's last birthday. Nobody mentioned it at the time, but Franklin knew he should have been there, so he asked his mother why father hadn't come.

"I'm sure I couldn't say," mother said to him.

"He's probably not flush enough," sister Rose said. She was married and lived nearby, so she came to the house often to see mother.

"The least he could do is send him a quarter card . . . or even write him a letter!" mother said. Then she set her jaw and went out of the living room, and Franklin was left alone with sister, who was staring straight ahead with her eyebrows raised, the smoke from her cigarette going right up over her head.

Franklin knelt on the couch and watched for father's long Chrysler from the front window. Sister Rose was with him on purpose, to be there when father came, since, of course, mother had gone into her bedroom and locked the door about an hour before, as she always did before father came for a visit.

She had wiped Franklin's face with a washcloth one last time, and said to sister, "Rose, keep him clean, will you?" And then she had said to Franklin, "Behave for your father, Franklin." He said he would—he always behaved when father came, and mother sucked her cheek and said, "You've had everything . . . and you've had nothing," before she set her jaw and went into her room. The lock on the door snapped loudly. Franklin went into the living room to wait with sister, hoping father would be flush this time to make up for the last birthday.

He didn't recognize the car at first, because it turned out that father had a new one. "I just throw 'em on the scrap heap when they get used up, sonny," he told him.

When Franklin opened the front door for him, father picked him up and scratched his face with his moustache, and squeezed his ribs, saying, "How's my littlest guy? You been a good boy? You all set to go back to school, are you? By golly though, you don't look like you've grown a mite though . . . do you clean your plate up good?"

"New car?" sister asked him when he set Franklin back down.

"Oh sure," father said, "got to keep up appearances."

"Paid for?" sister asked. Father, with a look very much like mother's, didn't answer her. "Are you in condition to drive it?" sister asked then, her eyebrows raised.

"That's no way to talk in front of him, Rose," father said, "little pitchers—" Franklin knew: they have big ears. When he complained of having big ears, mother always told him he'd grow up to them.

"Where are you taking him today?" sister asked.

"Out to buy him some school things!" father said loudly. "It's okay if the boy's father buys him a few things, isn't it!" Franklin, standing between them, could have reached out and touched them both on the belly button at the same time. He bet mother could hear in the bedroom, it was so loud.

"He hardly knew he had one on his birthday," sister said. Ever since brother Dick had left college and gone to New York to work for father, Rose talked about father with her eyebrows up. But if they were going out to buy school things, then father must be flush.

"Let's go, little man," father said, taking his hand with the two brown fingers from smoking. He saw father had a new ring.

"Get him home by six for supper, please," sister said, "and tell Dick he might try writing to his mother once in a while."

Sitting in the new Cadillac, Franklin held his feet straight out until father put his hand on his knees and said, "Don't. You'll get marks all over the dash." He couldn't think of anything to say just then, so he just sat and looked at the decorations in the new car. There was a coat of arms on every door, on the dash, and on the steering wheel, and father said that whenever it got hot, he could just turn on an air conditioner.

"Do you miss your brother Dick?" father asked him. When he said yes, he did, father said, "Well he lives with me in New York, you know, he works right for me now. I bet you'd like that!" Father didn't say anything more for a while, and Franklin tried, but he couldn't think of anything, until finally he remembered.

"I had a birthday," he said.

"Yes, I know," father said, and then he smoked a couple of times, and just when Franklin was about to ask him when they were going to buy the school things, father stopped the car and said, "Let's stop in here for a minute." They got out, and Franklin took hold of father's two brown smoking fingers, and father looked down from way up and said, "Hang on tight—can't have you getting hurt," as they crossed the busy street and went into a tavern.

"Alley Oop!" father said, lifting him up on a stool. The man came and grinned at Franklin and winked. "Give us a schnappser," father said, "and how about some soda for my boy."

Father had several schnappsers before Franklin could get the soda even half done.

The man came over again, and after father told him he could catch one for himself, the man snapped his fingers under Franklin's nose and said, "I guess that's too big a drink for a guy your size, squirt!" Father laughed and drank his schnappser and told the man that was his youngest—he had one boy—big guy used to play basketball at the university—working for him in New York. "Gonna play ball someday?" the man asked him. Then, "Better start sprouting if you wanna be big as your Pop someday!" Father laughed and he and the man had another schnappser.

"That's one hell of a ring you got there!" the man said.

Father held it out for him to see. "Something to pawn when I need my fur coat," father said, "but it's got a nigger in it—see right there?" and the man looked close at the ring, leaning to one side to get the light, and said yes, he saw the nigger, but it was still one hell of a ring for all that.

The man went away then, and Franklin worked at the soda while father smoked and pared his nails with a silver knife that had *Pete* engraved on the blade. Then father stepped away from the bar and looked at him for a while, and finally said, "You learn to really swim yet?"

"No," Franklin said, afraid that father would be angry. The last time they went to the cottage, he had told father he could swim, so father threw ten silver dollars off the deep end of the pier and told him to swim and get them. He tried, but it began to go dark as the evening came on, and brother Dick had to fish him out of the water, and father had said to hell with the ten dollars, leave them there if he was going to lie to his own father, and Franklin had been ill most of the night from swallowing lake water.

"Tell you what," father said now, clapping the silver knife together and dropping it in his pocket with all the change, "we'll go and buy us just the best damned back-to-school suit money can buy in this town, and then we'll go see Carl Case at his restaurant, how about that?"

"Who's Carl Case, father?" Franklin asked.

"Why!" father said, "Carl Case—I knew Carl Case when he was smaller than you—Yes sir!" father said. "We'll get all kinds of things you need, and then you come along and just ask Carl Case if he doesn't remember me when I was your size! Know what? I'm gonna buy you just a damn fine blue suit!"

"Watch out for your old man there, squirt," the man said from behind the bar; "don't let him get you in trouble!"

"You bet!" father said as they left.

The department store had big signs that said *BACK TO SKOOL TOGS*, and *SKOOL DAZE*, and many pictures of rulers, and children skipping and carrying books, and slates with sums on them. Father said they'd get the suit first, and then all the trimmings.

The man said, "You can't get a better suit . . . my own boys wear them."

"That's no recommendation!" father said, poking the man in the chest with a brown forefinger. "Is it the best blue suit I can buy? That's all, is it the best blue suit I can buy?" Then they had trouble about making it fit.

"I can't get alterations now, you have to leave it, sir," the man said.

"I'll be goddamned!" father said, "the little man wants to wear the suit right out of the store—he's paying good money and he wants to wear it out, so damnit, get a cuff put on it!" The man went and got another man, and they finally agreed to just baste up the cuffs.

"Is that cash?" the man asked father, "or charge?"

"I'm not exactly traveling broke!" father said, and opened his wallet and gave the man money. Then he said, "Now you just show us where you keep the readin' and writin' materials, huh?"

They walked along the aisle, he and father, and father chose the things for him and gave them to Franklin to carry as they went along.

"Oh, paper!" father said, "got to have us some paper to write on," and he took so many pads of paper from the stack that Franklin dropped some of them. "Ruler?" father said, "for damn sure a ruler! Pens?" and he took a big fistful of pens and stuck them in Franklin's pockets. "Erasers? . . . Check! . . . Magic Writing Tablet? —erases itself? . . . Check! Golden Books? . . . Check! Library paste? . . . Check!" When Franklin told him why he was crying, father called another man and told him to for Christ's sake get them a shopping bag, and the man got a big one for Franklin. He told father that he was sure his arms were strong enough to carry the bag.

As a self-imposed punishment for crying, Franklin promised to make himself carry the shopping bag, no matter how heavy it got.

They left soon after that, and father drove the new Cadillac to Carl Case's restaurant. "He'll be in the bar I'll bet," father said when they got there, and he was right, because Carl Case, who was as big and as old as father, with very stong-looking arms, was behind the bar. It was very dark in the room, and candles burned at every table, and there were soft blue lights that seemed to flow right out of the corners of the walls, and there was a big fishnet over Franklin's head when he looked up after father lifted him onto the stool. Carl Case was bald and wore a bow tie.

"Pete, you sonofabitch!" Carl Case said when he shook hands with father.

"I swore I'd be damned if I didn't get down here to see you this time!" father said.

"What do you call this little fella . . . what's his name, little boy blue?" Carl Case asked, putting his hand on Franklin's head.

"That's Franklin—that's my shrimp," father said. "Won't let go of that bag of crap I bought him for school . . . stand up on the stool and show him your new suit, boy!" father said, "I think that little suit is the nuts on him!" Then father and Carl Case had schnapp-sers, and Carl Case gave Franklin a lime soda. He found a way to balance the heavy shopping bag on his lap while he drank the soda.

"Yes sir," Carl Case said, "I knew your old man when he was your size . . . you got a lot of growing to do to fit his shoes, buster!" Father laughed hard at that and said that he guessed Franklin was the runt of his litter.

"I've got Dick out in New York with me now, you know," father said.

"You don't say!" Carl Case said. They drank schnappsers then and father told Carl Case all about business in New York.

"Your old man's ripping them up in New York, boy, did you hear that? What do you think about that?" Carl Case asked him. Franklin could have told him he knew that his father was flush, but he wasn't sure he ought to. "You don't say one hell of a lot, do you?" Carl Case said.

"Can't you talk?" father asked him.

"Carl Case has strong-looking arms," Franklin said, to show that the cat hadn't got his tongue.

"Sonofagun! Did you hear that, Pete?" Carl Case said, laughing and holding out his big, bare forearms.

"What d'you mean?" father said, taking off his jacket and rolling up his sleeve. He made a fist and laid his arm on the bar in front of Franklin. "What the hell's wrong with your old man's arm! Answer me, damnit! Is there anything wrong with your old man's arm?" he said. Franklin shook his head no, because he was afraid he'd cry if he tried to speak, and he'd promised himself not to do that again.

"Where'd you ever get a handle like Franklin for him, Pete?" Carl Case asked.

"Oh!" father said, "that's his mother's doing—she had to name him after her squarehead of an old man."

"Franklin?" Carl Case asked, pouring more schnappsers.

"Franklin! I guess Franklin!" father said.

"What, father?" Franklin said. Carl Case laughed at that.

"I wasn't talking to you," father said, "and why can't you call me Pete? Your brother Dick calls me Pete . . . let's hear you call me Pete once," he said, leaning his face down close to Franklin.

First Franklin pretended to have trouble holding the shopping bag on his lap, but then, when father took hold of his chin with his two brown smoking fingers and made him look right at him he had to shake his head no and refuse. "What's wrong?" father said, "your mother tell you not to call me Pete? Call me Pete just once! Your brother Dick does . . . won't you say it just once?"

Then father let go of his chin and said the hell with it, he was his mother's son, wasn't he. "She still the same way, Pete?" Carl Case asked.

"Christ on a crutch!" father said. "See that blue suit I bought the kid? That's the best, bestest bluest suit money can buy in this town . . . do you even like your new blue suit I bought you?" he asked Franklin. Franklin was going to say yes, he did, but the shopping bag really did begin to slip this time, and he grabbed for it, and his lime soda spilled into his lap. "Oh Christ!" father said.

"We'll just wipe that up and it'll be good as new," Carl Case said, getting a cloth.

Franklin didn't remember falling asleep. He remembered that father had rolled his sleeve back down, and he and Carl Case were having more schnappsers . . . and there was a faint echo in his memory of Carl Case saying, "I ought to get my waitresses to wear blue, Pete, it looks good as hell what with the lights."

He was lying on the seat of one of the booths in Carl Case's restaurant when he woke up. A policeman was leaning over him, looking closely at him, his mouth moving as though he were chewing gum. "This *is* your boy, isn't it?" the policeman said, and when he straightened up, the leather of the booth creaked and groaned where the policeman rested his hand. Franklin was sweating from his sleep, and his new blue suit . . . bluer than the policeman's uniform, chafed him at his throat and wrists, and his blue woolly trousers had drawn up hotly around his crotch while he slept.

"She's sending cops now, Carl," father said, "she's sending the goddamn gestapo after me now . . . I committed a crime, I took my boy out for the day . . . I'm a goddamned criminal!" Father was still at the bar, standing up. Another policeman was holding him by the arm.

"This boy was supposed to be home at six o'clock," the first policeman said. "If this boy's in his mother's custody, then the law says you get him home by when she says so." Then the policeman helped Franklin to sit up, and said to him, "What's your name, boy?"

"Franklin. That's my father," he said, pointing.

"No, no!" father said, "don't say I'm your father . . . if I'm your father, then I'm a criminal . . . my name's just plain Pete, and I don't know the kid, officer!"

"Now, Pete," Carl Case said from behind the bar, "the officer don't mean to call you that."

"Let's go home, boy," the policeman said, getting Franklin to stand on the floor. He felt the pins and needles of sleep in his legs. He clenched and extended his fingers, feeling his skin sticky. His new blue suit seemed to heat his body, hotter and hotter, until he had to squirm his toes inside his shoes to keep from taking off his jacket.

"Yes," father said, "let's go see what kind of a criminal I am!" But Franklin wouldn't go along with the policeman until he had found his shopping bag of school supplies. He might have slept again in the squad car on the way home, but he couldn't be sure. The shopping bag was still in his hands when the policeman opened the door of the squad car for him to get out, making the dome light go on.

"Upsy-daisy!" the policeman said, and took him by the hand and led him up the walk to his front door. Franklin thought that the two of them, he and the big policeman, were nearly invisible in the darkness of the night as they went up the walk, dressed in bluest blue. Then father's new Cadillac drove up behind the squad car, and another policeman got out and went around and opened the door for father, and he heard father say, "The condemned man ate a hearty meal."

Then all of them were in the front hall. Sister Rose had her hands on her hips, yelling at father, and brother Bob was there too, from all the way across town. There was no doubt but that mother could hear it in the bedroom. Franklin wondered if she came out while he and father were gone, or if she stayed in there until father was gone away for good, until the next time for a big splash.

"The police, Rose?" father was saying, "the police you had to call on me? Did you think I'd run off with him? Did you?" Father tried to touch Rose, but she pushed him away, and stumbling backwards, one of the policemen brushed Franklin into the corner next to the umbrella rack, where he stood alone, and watched, and listened.

"You haven't bought the right to put your hands on me!" Rose yelled, her eyebrows raised. The policeman told her not to yell.

"That's all you want . . . why didn't you just tell the cops to bring my wallet home, save me the trouble of a trip . . . next time I'll just send you a check, Rose!" father said.

"All right, let's don't have any of this—" the policeman began to say, but father wouldn't let him finish.

"Here," father said, "here! Take it and put it in hock, I'm a little short for cash!" he said. And father twisted off the big diamond ring from his brown smoking finger and threw it, and it hit brother Bob in the neck. There's a nigger in it, there's a nigger in it! Franklin wanted to say from his dark front-hall corner. They were all so big and loud. He seemed to be looking out and up at them from the bottom of a deep, dark hole . . . a dark, warm, itchy hole that grew hotter and hotter.

"You bastard!" brother Bob said, and the policeman tried to stop him, but Bob was too fast, and he hit father with his fist, and father fell back against Franklin, nearly crushing him under his weight and the bulky, sharp-edged weight of the heavy shopping bag that Franklin still held. Brother Bob yelled "Ow!" when the first policeman grabbed his arm and put a chain on his wrist and twisted it.

"That'll be enough, that'll just be enough!" the policeman said.

Father spit blood on the front-hall floor and said, "You forgot I was still your father after all . . . the hell with you!"

"You ruin, you ruin everything," Rose said, crying.

"Come on now," the policeman said to Bob, "You didn't want to do anything like that."

"Dad, Dad," brother Bob said, "I didn't mean that . . . I didn't mean that, Dad," and he put his free hand out to father.

"Ah bullshit!" father said, "all you want's the money . . . don't give me the Dad crap, I'm no father, I'm plain old Pete . . . if I'm Dad I go to jail for a criminal," father said, and he started to push his way past the other policeman toward the outside door.

"Don't be an ass!" sister Rose said, still crying.

"I'm sorry I hit you, Dad," Bob said, trying to reach father with his hand.

"I answer to the name of Pete, and I haven't got any more money, so you'll all have to wait!" father said.

"Now Pete, easy does it, huh?" the other policeman said.

"I'm not Dad—the goddamn hell with Dad!" father said, on the front porch now, the other policeman helping him with the first steps.

Then mother came running into the front hall, and the first policeman and Rose and Bob had to hold her from going out after father. "Get out! Get out!" she screamed, her voice breaking through the dark night, covering the sound of the big, full shopping bag hitting the front hall floor, its sides splitting, pencils, pens, paper, sliding across the tiles. . . .

Covering the sound of Franklin's voice, as he spoke, his hands raised toward the front door, only his hands and the rich, blue wool cuffs of his jacket sleeves sticking out of the dark corner where he stood next to the umbrella rack . . . "Pete," he said, "Pete. . . ."

Granger Hunting

"Daddy, there, look," the boy said. Granger instinctively brought the Winchester to his shoulder. In the reverie he conducted within himself, he'd imagined how he'd react if a deer crossed their path on the way back to the cabin to save the day for him.

Granger spun in the direction his son pointed, the rifle's sights splitting the chest of the deer where it stood just outside the range of thick pines on Granger's property. "There," his son shouted again, forgetting himself, running through the snow toward the deer. The deer lurched back to the cover of pines just as Granger fired and he knew it was gutshot, not a killing shot. They'd have to trail it. He fired once more, the sound of the 30-30 cracking the freezing air, aiming for the flag of the deer's tail as it jumped once, stiffly graceful, over a windfallen log, then was gone.

"Did you miss again?" the boy asked him, reminding Granger of the squirrel he had missed as it sat on the trunk of a pine. The boy had been complaining of the cold, doubting there was any game at all to be seen in the woods. Granger emptied his rifle at the squirrel to show him that a man could go out in the woods with a gun and actually see and kill game, even if only a squirrel.

"Not by a damn sight," Granger said, smiling. "We'll get him." He led the boy over to where the deer had stood. There was blood on the snow, the cloven tracks disturbed where the animal thrashed for a second as the dum-dum tore into its stomach, then a break in the brush where it entered the pine cover. "Did you see the rack on him boy?" Granger said.

"I just looked up and there he was," the boy said, "like he was watching us. Do you think a deer knows you're trying to kill him when he sees you?" His son scuffed fresh snow over the spots of blood, then seemed lost again in the silence that so easily irritated Granger. It made him feel foolish, as if he were dragging a stuffed doll of a boy through the woods with him.

"They don't think like people," Granger said. "All they know is to run when someone comes close to them or when they're hit. Now we have to go get him."

"Follow him?"

"We'll sit and wait for a while. Give him a chance to think we've quit. He'll lay down in the snow and bleed. Then we can get near him." They found a spot inside the pines where the sharp wind had picked a large rock clean of snow. Granger took out the pint he carried against the cold. "Do you want to warm your insides?" he asked the boy, no longer afraid to offer him a drink of whiskey because of what his mother might say when his son was home, telling her about the hunt with his father. Now everything was easier.

"I don't like the taste of that stuff."

"Suit yourself. It warms you." He drank. He wiped his lips and moustache on the sleeve of his red parka, capped the bottle and slipped it inside, into the breast pocket of his wool shirt. He cradled the rifle in his arms, cupped his hands and lit a Pall Mall with the lighter he'd made himself, years before, on a lathe . . . when his boys were young and he worked, worked steady, all through the Depression as a machinist in a small shop on Chicago's south side. "That's more than fifteen years old," he said more to himself than to the boy, rubbing his thumb gently over his name, cut into the heavy-gauge steel by a friend in the shop who did a little engraving on the side.

"It's colder just sitting here so long," his son said. "It'll get dark soon. We can't hunt after dark, can we?"

"We've got all night if we need it," Granger said. "Won't it frost your brothers when we come dragging a five- or six-point buck in? I guess you don't have to be an Indian to get a deer, do you?" he said, remembering Smythe. And then he did it again. In the moment when Granger was ready to think, yes, everything was working out fine, then his youngest son spoke petulantly, selfishly, and tore the insides from him, took away the satisfaction he felt, left him hollow with weariness of himself.

"Can't we just let the deer go?"

"No we can't," Granger said loudly, the sound echoing as the shots from his rifle had echoed. "You think it's cruel to hunt? My god, the cruelest thing is to shoot an animal and then let it go off in the woods and die slow. Wolves gang up on an injured deer and bring it down. Is that what you want? You want it to die of starvation? It's shot in the belly, gutshot. It's hurt so it can't eat anything. We've got to find it and finish it off." For emphasis he slapped the large case knife he carried to cut the throat of downed deer, open them, dress them out. He stood up and spat his cigarette end into the snow. "Let's go, he'll be laying down now. We'll just crawl up slow on him."

"At least it's over after today," his son said.

"That's right. That's fine," Granger said. "Tomorrow your brothers can take you home and you won't have to run around the woods with your old man any more. That's just fine."

"I didn't mean it that way."

"Let's go," Granger said. Now it didn't matter if the boy enjoyed it or not. He'd shot his deer and he meant to track him, finish him, haul him into the deer shack's yard so the older boys could see him bring it in. He'd hang the carcass up on the two-by-four nailed to two trees, let it drip clean, freeze overnight. In the morning his boys could get in their rattle-trap Plymouth and drive back to Chicago to their mother. Granger would rope the deer to the roof of his new Chrysler, back to Minneapolis with him.

They cut through the heavy brush and windfall, skirting the pine stands. Granger was already delivering the deer to the locker plant in St. Paul. It came back, wrapped, the cuts of meat labeled. This time he'd cook it himself because Flossie, his second wife, didn't know how to prepare venison properly. He'd throw a big dinner for someone, friends, men from his firm in Minneapolis.

"It's getting colder," his son said behind him.

"Don't lag," Granger said, "and damnit, don't whine!" The deer was easy to follow, losing a lot of blood now. It wasn't going to be far.

It was the last of deer season. That morning he and the boy stood outside the deer shack waiting for his brothers to come out so they could start. "You ready to get a deer today boy?" Granger asked. His son ran his bare fingers over the deep uneven grooves raked into the boards by a wandering black bear that spring. The bear either felt the desire to test his claws after the inactivity of hibernation or perhaps smelled the past year's scent of bacon and beef in the cabin. "You'd better put those mittens on quick, son," Granger said. The boy didn't answer, but abandoned the damage done by the bear and put on the red mittens Granger had brought from Minneapolis for him. They were bright, deer hunter's red, reached up to the middle of the boy's forearms. Granger's second wife, Flossie, had never had children, wasn't much of a knitter; Granger meant to tell her she'd made them too big. That's tomorrow, Granger thought—it'll be over tomorrow.

"Why didn't you put the horns up over the door when you got a deer?" the boy asked him.

"I guess I never got around to it," Granger said. "I left a six-point rack outside the cabin here two years ago. When I came back for some fishing in the spring the porcupines had chewed it up for the minerals." He was prepared to go on, explain the porcupine's need for salt, but his son turned away. Granger reached into the cartridge pocket of the heavy hunting parka for the six bullets he'd been loading into his Winchester each morning of deer season, removing each evening. The brass cases were icy against his fingers. The dum-dum heads felt like lumps of frozen earth, filed smooth.

"Well," he said, "are we going to get us one today? This is it, now or never." He smiled, his dentures still chilled from sitting in the metal cup half full of water during the night. The fire in the belly of the oil-drum stove went out sometime before the Big Ben alarm woke them, and the shack was bitterly cold as they dressed.

Granger was the first one up, proud of that. After building a fire in the stove, he dressed, found his cigarettes, smoked for a few moments, listening to the sound of his three sons breathing, still fast asleep.

He dipped two fingers into the water in the metal cup, slipped the icy dentures into his mouth. He set the upper plate fast against his palate with his tongue; the cold attacked his gums, made his jaws ache—for an instant he wanted to undress, get back into the lower bunk bed with his youngest boy while the stove thawed the air in the cabin.

But the sun brought a dull grayness tinted with orange at the edges of the sky, and besides, he hadn't gotten his deer yet this year; nobody had even seen one. The sun coming up was a vague but real promise of possibilities, awakening anticipations, offering a chance. He might this day get his deer, he might this day push a finger through the wall between himself and his sons. Touch them. He might miss something that would never be offered again if he went back to bed.

"Let's go hunting," he said to his youngest son when he gently shook him awake. The boy blinked, sat up, frowned.

"Is it time already?" Granger stood over him, made himself look kindly, not saying: You come all the way up north from Chicago to go deer hunting with your father, how often do you get a chance to see your father, much less a chance to hunt the best deer country in Wisconsin? Millionaires try to buy into the land around here for hunting and fishing. How often do you get a chance like that?

But the boy was still groggy, too drugged with the last moments of his sleep for argument or logic, impervious to his father. Granger turned away, stepped up on the first rung of the bunk ladder to shake the older boys awake.

He lit the kerosene stove and put water on to boil for coffee, the cabin warming now. He set out groceries for breakfast, cleared the rough wood table of cribbage board, cards, ashtrays, the porcelain cups they drank whiskey from the night before. He watch his sons dress.

He tried to see them naked infants once more, to feel the father's right to put his hands on them as he had so many times years ago. This was difficult, both to do and to realize its difficulty as he did it, so he made breakfast preparations as he watched them, pretended that breakfast was important.

Phil was quiet, dressing quickly and efficiently, wasting no motion. Al complained he had a hangover from his whiskey the night before when Granger had been giving them object lessons in cribbage. The little boy, Mack Jr., whimpered, pale with cold and discomfort after he stripped off his pajamas and tried to force a thin white leg into the longjohns Granger had bought for him in Minneapolis when he shopped for hunting supplies. That was his mother's doing, Granger thought, that the boy insisted on sleeping in pajamas.

He looked at his older boys, adultly distant, resistant to all but the things Granger could give them, do for them. They grew up, grew away from him during the war. They were too old when Granger and his wife were divorced, knew too much ever to trust him again. But the little one, Mack, Mack Jr., Granger thought—delighted as though it were a new discovery, for he never thought himself as Mack Granger Sr. He might still touch the little boy.

"The sooner we get out there the sooner we'll get back," Al said as he came out of the shack with Phillip. He smoked a too-long cigar, rolling it from side to side in his mouth, reminding Granger of a certain Jewish lawyer who had something to do with handling the divorce for Anne. The two older boys looked like patchwork scarecrows, long strips of thin red cloth safety pinned to their G.I. fatigue jackets.

Granger felt suddenly foolish, ostentatious in his expensive hunting gear. He'd snapped the metal deer tag through a buttonhole, and Flossie stitched the strip of red cloth bearing his license number to the middle of the parka's back. He felt like a tourist photographed while wearing sunglasses, an aloha shirt, a box camera on a strap hanging around his neck. Yet he knew if he ever traveled to Hawaii that's just how he'd dress.

"It's the coldest yet this morning," Phil said. "Maybe Mack should stay back here in the cabin." Granger smiled, expected the boy to protest loudly, immediately. When he only kicked at the packed snow and watched some snowbirds flitting near Granger's Chrysler, parked next to the cabin and hung with fresh nocturnal snow, Granger spoke quickly.

"Hell, I need a good man to help me drag my deer in. Right? Son?"

"If there's even any deer around here at all," the boy said.

"Certainly there's deer around here," Granger said too loudly. "I told you I got my deer last year just behind the shack. I told you that, boy," he said, and then was aware he was trying to bully the boy into it, shout down any request he might make to stay back at the cabin.

"You want to go out and freeze your can off today?" Al said, giving the boy a mock swat on the rear.

"Do you want to go with your Dad?" Phil asked him soberly. He looked up at Granger while they waited for the boy to answer. Granger read the determination to allow the boy to choose for himself in Phil's eyes. Granger bargained.

"You can carry the compass," he said, unbuckling the strap that held it on his wrist like a watch. He took the boy's arm in his two hands, strapped the compass to his wrist. He was bribing, and if it had been necessary or rational he'd have pulled out his wallet and stacked money on the snow in front of the boy. He'd give him his rifle, offer him the deed to the cabin, mortgage all possibilities and sureties and aspirations for this one affirmation from him.

"Make up your mind," Phillip said harshly, disinterested; "we don't have all day." Granger resented the tone. Only his father ought to speak to the boy that way; Phil's voice said clearly that Granger no longer had that right.

From a distance in the woods they heard six rapid shots. "That's the Indian," Granger said, falling on it as though it were a wild trump card. "Listen to that old Garand he carries. He's out there in the woods already, boy. I doubt if we'll get through the day without running into him. Remember me telling you about the Indian I got this land from?"

"I'll go with him," the boy said; he stepped across the line Granger had drawn in his imagination between himself and his two older boys, one only the young boy was young and ignorant enough to cross. I have rights, Granger thought. I'm the boy's father.

"Take care of yourself, Mack," Phil said, as if Granger didn't know how. It was easy to hate children when they grew up.

"Let's get moving before we freeze to the spot," Al said. He and Phil moved off toward the woods.

Granger and the boy stood at the cabin until they were nearly out of sight. "Come on," Granger said, "I'll show you how to get a deer." They went down the road running past the cabin, looking for a good point to cut into the woods. Granger showed his son how they couldn't get lost in the woods so long as they had the compass. Even without a compass they could steer by the sun if the day were clear. Granger told him the story of how Smythe, the Indian, found two men in the spring who'd been lost the winter before. Not a pretty sight—Granger omitted the details that could have frightened the boy.

They passed the *No Trespassing* signs Granger had posted on his land. His spirits freshened and he became confident when he saw the *by order of owner* that meant him, his indelible mark: Mack Granger. A good feeling. He turned off the road, and moving ahead of his son, broke the trail through the dead brush and deep snow for the boy. He felt he could hunt for hours without flagging, positive they wouldn't leave the woods until he had his deer. They found a game trail and Granger called a halt. "We'll sit here a while and something's liable to walk right past us."

"Do you think we'll really see the Indian?"

"Never tell for sure," he said, and because the subject of the Indian interested the boy, went on, "He's a hell of a hunter. He carries that heavy Garand through the brush like it was nothing. The Indians around here eat deer meat all year round you know."

"Isn't it against the law?"

"Lots of things are," Granger said. It sounded too cynical, something the boy's mother wouldn't like him saying to their son. He changed the subject. "It's kind of a shame the season's over with today. When we're just getting going good. You think you're going to like hunting, do you?"

"It's not much fun when you can't carry a gun."

"You have to be fourteen to carry a gun in Wisconsin. That's the law," Granger said. His son looked at him, and only after the boy turned away, shivering and huddling into the parka his father had bought for him, did Granger realize how he'd contradicted himself. He wanted to drop his rifle in the snow, embrace his son, both warm him with his body and make him see that hypocrisy was only reality, that in time he would understand all this. But he was afraid to say anything that would sound funny to the boy's mother in the telling.

Granger spat into the snow, then took the pint of whiskey he always carried against the cold when hunting. He taunted the boy's legal allegiance to his mother. "Have a snort of this," he said, "it'll warm you."

"Whiskey?"

"Go on, it'll be our secret." He was glad when the boy took the pint and drank from it, as though he'd scored a point. His son sneezed, wiped at his eyes.

"It burns."

"Give it a minute," Granger said. They heard the Indian's Garand, four shots this time, and Granger was glad to trade a knowing glance with his son. Knowledge shared. He despaired, though, of being able to find something to say or do that would entertain the boy. He had visions of himself doing headstands, somersaults in the deep snow to amuse him. Pessimism crept into him with the intense cold; Granger almost laughed at himself.

"I'm still cold. That whiskey doesn't work."

"Try to stop thinking about it, it only makes it worse." He opened the pint and took a longer drink. It did burn. The last day was off to a bad start.

The wounded deer was easy to trail. At first the blood was slight because it was moving so fast, still in shock from the bullet that had ripped its stomach. Then it had slowed because no one was following. They had sat wisely, Granger knew. The blood increased. They found where the deer had finally stopped, the warmth of its body forming a deep hollow in the snow lined red with bleeding. Buck put his bare hand to it, the spot still warm.

"That sucker didn't get up long ago," Granger said, surprised at the wheezing in his voice. He'd been pushing it too fast; a hardness formed in his chest. He held his breath, heard the blood pound in his ears, felt it move near his temples.

"How can he bleed so much and still keep running? I'm tired, Dad," his son said.

"They can go a long ways and still carry lead in them. He's heading back into the swamps, the bastard—" he caught the profanity on his lips, tried too late to swallow it back. "We'll rest here a while and he'll lay down again. One of these times he won't be able to get up.

Over here," he said, and he brushed snow from a windfallen log for
them to sit on.

"I'm cold. I can't even feel my toes any more, Dad. Can't we go
home?" Granger found something to divert him.

"Look over there, there's some more sign of the game you said you
didn't think there was in this woods. This place is full of wildlife.
Just look at that."

"What is it?"

"That's a kill. That's an owl kill. A rabbit. See the little balls of
fur? They eat everything, then vomit the fur in those little balls. A
rabbit, see, there's the head." The owl's kill was old, the balls of
rabbit fur, the rabbit's head, the owl's feces all dusted with snow.
Granger kicked the rabbit head toward the boy to convince him; the
boy turned away. "What's the matter?"

"I don't like it. Let's go back, Dad. I don't care if we catch the
deer or not. I don't care if he does die slow. Let's please go back."

"What the hell's the matter with you?" Granger shouted, not just
to his son, but farther, to the woods, the whole of the universe, to
everything not working for him or with him. He heard only his own
echo roll in the trees. His son kept his back to him. He blamed it on
his first wife, on the distance that had existed between Minneapolis
and Chicago since the divorce, when the boy was seven. "What do
you think owls eat for breakfast? Corn flakes? Look at it. Look at it
for Christ's sakes, will you? How the hell will you ever be able to do
anything if this makes you sick? What kind of a pantywaist are you?
Damnit boy." Still he wouldn't turn to him.

Granger quit. "Come on, we'll move a little further up to wait.
Your feelings won't be hurt five minutes from now. What's the use,"
he said to the forest.

They went away from the owl's kill and the spot where the deer
had lain down to bleed and die in peace until it heard them coming.
Granger wiped away his concern for his son, for everything, and
compressed his purpose in life down to the proportions of the deer he
was not going to leave without killing. He knew the animal would
seek its quiet place to die and he meant to find it there.

"How much longer will it be?" his son asked.

"A while. Give him time to start dying."

There'd been shaky going on the roads north of Minneapolis, snow flurries that slicked the highway treacherously and made it play at whipping Granger's new Chrysler into a deadly ditch or bridge abutment. It had been near midnight, four days ago, when he drove up to the deer shack. His sons sat in the battered Plymouth, the heater malfunctioning, maintaining a temperature just a shade warmer than the heavy black air of the woods. They were all too strained and tired to be glad to see each other again. From the beginning it went badly.

"Why the hell didn't you just kick the lock off and go on in and get the stove going, it'll throw enough heat to drive you outside," Granger raged in a minor key.

"How should we know you want your lock forced or not?" Phil answered evenly.

"Kee-rist," Al said, "let's get in and get a fire going now. Did you bring anything to drink, Popper?"

"How've you been keeping yourself, boy?" Granger asked his youngest son. The boy was too old to kiss now. A handshake would have been comic in the frozen night.

"I'm cold," the boy said, then followed his brothers into the cabin that was colder than the outdoors until the oil-drum stove had been stoked with the briquets Buck had in the trunk of the Chrysler.

"I'm cold," he'd said this morning as they waited at the game trail. Granger opened his eyes, needles raining on his feet and the tips of his fingers. Had he dozed? They shook off the snow sticking to their boots, moved back down the game trail to the road. "How could anything be alive in this weather?" his son said. Then Granger saw the squirrel.

It was only about thirty yards away, upside down on the trunk of a thick pine tree. It clung rigidly to the base of the pine, its soft tail raised like an umbrella or antenna over its head, as though listening for enemies in the forest. Granger pulled back the hammer on the Winchester. "Quiet," he said to his son, and "Watch this."

Granger took it as a lucky break, a chance to make interesting again the game of hunting that so disappointed his son. And for him, lucky for him too.

He intended to explode the squirrel, expected to see him evaporated by the 30-30 dum-dum slug, thus demonstrating that one could hunt, could go into a sameness of snow, trees, and brush, find wild game there, take conscious aim and kill, prove that a form of life, more ancient than the racial memories of the drunken and thieving Indians who were the only year-long residents of the area, was still a real and viable form for grown men of means to follow with satisfaction. He tried to prove that sense and purpose still prevailed and that all things still came to him who waited.

He fired, missed, saw the pine bark jump to the right of the squirrel, expected the animal to disappear in fright, but it remained, confused, only changing the cant of its head, the raised angle of its quivering tail.

"You missed," his son said.

"The little sucker doesn't know what the hell's up," Granger said. He levered another round into the chamber and raised to sight. The dum-dum struck just below the squirrel's head, the bark popping up in its face, exposing the fresh raw wood to the clear, bitter air. Granger cursed. He fired the remaining four rounds quickly, frenzied, feeling the unsureness of his aim, the cold coming through his trigger-finger mitten to make his squeeze uncertain. The butt jammed sharply into his shoulder with each shot, and the bullets struck farther from the squirrel. The last round made the snow fly at the base of the tree; the squirrel clattered to the opposite side of the pine trunk.

His son knelt to scoop up the brass casings for souvenirs where each empty shell had cut its form imperfectly into the soft surface of white powder snow. Granger let the rifle droop, as empty himself as the weapon, left after the repeated heat of firing and missing with a hollow appreciation of his own incapacities, and with a taste for nothing more than a certain expectation of nonfulfillment yet to come.

"Don't you have to reload?" the boy asked him as Granger led the way along a trail he'd blazed earlier.

"We'll go back to the road and go down further before we work our way in again." On the road they met Smythe, the Indian, who walked tall as a tower, the heavy Garand slung soldier-like, seeming impudently unaware of the cold.

Granger and the Indian shook hands. "Hello, Smythe," he said. "We heard you popping away out there. What happened to you? Miss?" Granger relaxed, expanded. With another adult, with the Indian, there was an eternal due of deference, collectable whenever convenient.

"How are you, Mr. Granger. Oh, I got him all right, but it was a her. A doe. I dressed it and hung it on a tree. I'll go back after dark when the warden isn't around the next bend and bring her in for cabin meat."

"This is a spike-buck season," the boy said, "does are illegal."

"That they are," Smythe said, smiling slightly.

Embarrassed, Granger spoke quickly. "Son, I want you to shake hands with Jack Smythe," and seeing his son shake with the Indian made him feel as if he'd taught the boy something of manners, something he'd need to function in this world. "This is my youngest son, my little guy."

"Doesn't seem so small to me," Jack said, paying part of the debt, Granger expanding with the security born in good business practice.

"Hell," Granger said, "they grow fast. I've got a boy in his late twenties. This one's twelve—"

"I'm thirteen," his son interrupted. The two men smiled at Granger's mistake and Granger changed the subject, afraid to trust himself with the names and ages of his other sons now.

"You still shooting the game for your clients?" Granger asked him. The Indian reached into his pocket, drew out a handful of the metal deer tags.

"I've got about half of them taken care of."

"Where the hell do you find them? We haven't seen anything except the snowbirds."

"We saw a squirrel," the boy said.

"I heard firing over on your land just before," Smythe said, "wasn't that you?"

"We were target practicing," the boy said. In the look Granger took from his son he understood that the boy was lying for him. It could have been a proof of love, as he wanted it to be, or a sign of obligation, which he didn't want.

"The deer are all mostly back in the swamps. Snow drove them back, Mr. Granger," the Indian said. "You have to really tramp in there if you want one."

"I don't think my boy could take the going in the woods in there, Jack." He turned to his son. "Unless you'd really like to get in there. You heard the man, we'd have to cut our way in if you really want to bag a deer. What do you say?" He hoped.

"Why don't we go back now and wait for Al and Phil, Dad," he said. "It's noon already, Dad. Let's give it up." Nothing. Nonfulfillment. Not one gesture, not one offer beyond the lie about the squirrel he'd missed with six shots at thirty yards.

"It's a goddamn shame," Granger said. The Indian shrugged, eased the heavy Garand off his left shoulder, transferred it and slung it on his right. Now, Granger thought, the goddamn weather drives the goddamn deer into the goddamn swamps. To hell with it!

"My feet are freezing, Dad," the boy said. "Those boots aren't any good in the snow."

"You got time for a drink or are you too interested in hunting?" Granger asked the Indian. He wasn't going to have his older boys find him in the cabin, boring himself with a pocket novel. No sir.

"Always time for a drink, Mr. Granger, you know me."

"Aren't we going back to the cabin?" his son asked.

"We're going to a tavern. You'll like it," Granger said, "it's full of stuffed animals. You like that?"

"I like them to look at I guess."

"Come on down to my place," Smythe said. "We'll take my jeep. I've got a storage battery with a jumper cable in case she's too stiff with cold to kick over."

They hiked three-quarters of a mile to the Indian's place, a lodge of pine logs, peeled, varnished, well built. Granger wanted to stick his head in the door and see if he knew any of the big-money boys who'd be there, men who took off for deer season, paid the Indian plenty, gave him their deer tags, then spent the days inside getting diarrhea from the Indian's cooking, playing poker for high stakes, boozing it. If the boy hadn't been with him he would have.

They had to use the jumper cable to get the jeep started. Granger told Smythe he ought to get himself a Chrysler; they were the nuts for starting in cold weather.

He settled for giving the Indian a drink from his pint while he drove. Granger finished the bottle, opening the side curtains of the jeep, the rushing wind bringing tears to his eyes, and hurling the empty pint into the snow piled at the side of the road by the county's plows.

Ed Sprague's tavern was a happy place for hunters and fishermen. It was closed during the off seasons, but otherwise very busy. The bartender went up and down behind the long bar, filling shot glasses and drawing glasses of beer. He hastily twisted paper bags around the necks of half-pints, pints, fifths for men like Granger, who wanted something to carry against the cold in the woods while they stalked game.

Stuffed wild animals peopled the corners of the room, arched in natural poses. A bobcat, dead for thirty years, snarled, one paw lifted, taken in the midst of a stroll. A squirrel like the one Granger failed to hit with his Winchester had stopped permanently in its path up the pine pole supporting the roof. A pair of mallard ducks flew at the ends of nearly invisible wires over the bar. On the wall, behind glass, stretched the world's record tiger muskie. It was over thirty inches at the girth, nearly six feet long. A hand-lettered sign said it had been caught by the owner of the bar and gave details of line weight, time consumed in beaching the fish, the date it was caught.

The bar, seen from the door, was a gallery of license numbers men's wives had sewn to the backs of their jackets. Cigarette smoke seemed to come out of the imitation knotty pine walls.

Granger and the Indian drank schnapps and the boy had orange soda pop. Granger introduced his son to the bartender and a couple of the customers he knew. After three drinks the Indian excused himself and went to the men's room.

"Did the man that owns this place shoot all these animals?" the boy asked Granger.

"I doubt it. The Indians, maybe even Smythe shot them for him."

"He must be a real hunter."

"They do it for the whiskey," Granger said. He would not have the boy admire the Indian. "It's against the law for him to sell liquor to an Indian. Didn't you know that? I thought you were so smart. You say you read a lot of books. What the hell do you read? Why do you think I buy all the drinks here? Smythe can't buy a legal drink in here."

"All I said was he was a good hunter." He turned away.

Granger wondered if the boy doubted the truth from his own father's lips. He hoped he'd merely hurt his feelings by referring to the books he read. "What I said is true about the law and selling liquor to Indians. Ask Smythe yourself when he gets back if you want."

"I believe you."

"I'm sorry about the hunting, boy," he said suddenly, without having planned it.

"That's okay," his son said. Granger was mortified, as if he was being forgiven a harmless vice. "I never thought I'd like hunting anyway."

"Not everybody does," Granger said. "There's other things in life. You know I'm trying to persuade your brothers to come up to the twin cities and work with me when they get this college business out of the way, don't you? Have you ever thought about that?" He knew the boy would talk of this to his mother, and she would hate Granger for it, but he didn't care any more. He waved to the bartender for another schnapps. Smythe returned to the bar in time for another drink.

"College is a good thing. I'm going to college," his son said.

"I never said it wasn't. It teaches you how to learn. Guys our age didn't have any G.I. Bill to send us off to school, did we, Smythe?" The Indian signaled agreement.

"Phil has some friends whose dads send them," the boy said.

"College is all right," Granger said. "But I've known a lot of characters who couldn't cut the mustard right out of college. Your brothers are going to get a break coming in with me when they're done with school. You should get educated for the kind of work you're going to do. If you're going to sell machinery, mining machinery, you can get some fairly specific courses in business. That's all I'm saying."

"Phil says he's going to be a teacher," his son said. The boy's lips were tight. Granger knew he was being defied; he hoped he was being lied to.

"He's what?"

"He's going to be a teacher. Ask him yourself if you don't believe me. I don't know what I want to be yet when I grow up," he said. Granger wanted to slap his face for daring to offer him this last as consolation.

"I believe you," he said. "Let's have another round, Jack. Out of the mouths of babes. Let's drink to long life, when you finally find out how things are in this world. My boy's going to be a teacher. Why do we have children, Jack, can you tell me that? That's my oldest boy, Phillip, you know. You have children, a man has children," he said. He blew his nose on the red hunter's handkerchief; pull out a white handkerchief in the woods and some fool hunter would see a deer's flag, blaze away at you. "You have them, but you can't talk to them. They don't tell you anything, Jack. Let's celebrate. The hell with it, to hell with the goddamn deer and the whole damn shooting match." He'd drunk enough so he couldn't feel the burn of the schnapps, and except for his dread of hangover in the morning he'd have gotten thoroughly drunk. Hangovers reminded him of death, the lingering helplessness of dying. When Smythe made his offer Granger knew it was simple gratitude. He'd done a few favors for the Indian in the past.

"I'll get you a deer if you want, Mr. Granger. It makes me no more trouble than not to. I've got to go out tonight and bring in the doe I killed. I can take a lantern and jack-light me a spike-horn for you."

Granger looked at his son, saw he watched closely. The worst would be if he were only curious, if he didn't care whether he took the offer or not.

"How about that? There's a chance to get us a deer. What do you think of that? Think of the trouble it'd save. No tromping in the woods after a deer." He looked out the window on the other side of the room, the sky overcast. "Probably too late now anyway for us. It's going to snow again tonight."

"It's against the law," his son said. Then he looked away, as if saying he couldn't be responsible for his father.

"I'd be glad to shoot you a deer, Mr. Granger. Just let me have your tag and I'll drop him right at your shack. No trouble at all."

Granger drank his schnapps. Sweet to his throat and tongue, it soured in his stomach, and he knew one more drink would leave him with a blinding headache in the evening. "Thank you but no thank you, Smythe," he said. "Let's go, boy. Take it easy now, Jack," he called back to the Indian.

He stopped at the door and pointed at the world's record muskie behind glass. "Don't let that thing fool you. Smythe keeps a dozen muskies in a pond, feeds them all year long, year after year, and when the boss man here needs a new world's record, Jack nets one for him. Don't let it fool you," he said, and forced a laugh out of the boy, slapping him on the shoulder, pushing him ahead, out through the door. The sky was a sure sign of snow. "We'll walk back. To hell with riding."

"Why didn't you let him get a deer for you, Dad?"

"When I want a deer bad enough I'll go get my own." But he didn't want anything. He didn't want a deer to impress his boys. He didn't want one for himself. They walked along the snow-packed road in silence, the boy huddling into his parka against the wind that rose now. Granger let the rifle droop in the crook of his arm. He wanted nothing and no one any more, so the cold barely bothered him, for there was no impulse or inspiration or anticipation or anything coming to him that could make him eager and warm again.

He walked that way, turned inward on his disappointments, brooding until it became pessimism, turned back to become faintly optimistic again, became a reverie in which he killed a deer and had sons who loved him.

They reached his own land, his son saw the deer, and they began to track it, winding deeper into the swampland. They followed the deer's bloody trail, the sky darkened, and snowflakes were drifting down through the pine branches when they finally caught it.

"There," Granger said, "easy now. We've got her." He pointed with his rifle and put his other arm in front of his son. "Hold this," he said without looking at the boy, handing him the Winchester.

"What do you have to do?" the boy said. He held the rifle away from his body with both hands on the stock, as though it were alive.

"Finish it." He slipped the case knife from its sheath. They'd waited long enough this time; the deer had lain down to die, but had not, for it lifted its head, looked at Granger, white-eyed, thrashing with its forefeet to get up again, uselessly, its strength gone.

"He's still alive, Daddy," his son said. The boy's voice was high-pitched. "Shoot it again, Daddy, do something, kill it, please."

"Shut up," Granger said. He circled around behind the deer. The animal slowly tried to twist its head a full one hundred and eighty degrees, keep him in sight. It snorted and coughed, but could not rise. "You have to be careful. They can cut you to ribbons with their feet and horns. Easy now," he said aloud, to himself. The deer groaned once, deeply, stretched its neck away from Granger, then toppled on its side.

Granger hopped, straddled the animal's neck, the horns slippery in his free hand. He pulled back, caught the deer's chin in his palm, stretched its neck for the knife. There was a rush of air from the deer's throat as he struck, then drew, and blood filled the path of the knife. The deer quivered in long spasms. Granger struck again with the knife, and his son screamed.

"Stop it, Daddy, *stop it stop it please!*"

"Quiet," Granger said. He dropped the deer's head and sprang away from it, expecting a final, most violent spasm to shake the animal. His stomach felt empty, weak with anticipating the lurching horns ripping into him. The animal died quickly. He went over to the boy and took the rifle away from him, stood it against a tree. "Now you're going to help me dress him out," he said. Now, Granger cared.

His sons could go back to their mother, the whole thing had been a bust, but he was going to drag his deer in, hang it in front of the shack to freeze overnight. He was going to go back to Minneapolis alone, but he was by Christ going to have that deer roped to his Chrysler.

The boy cried all through gutting the animal. Granger told him once to stop and blow his nose but he continued to kneel in the snow and hold the carcass for his father. The animal's blood froze to Granger's hands while sweat formed and stung at his face from the exertion. He unwound the dragging rope from around his waist, secured the carcass. When he looked up it was all but dark.

"Mack," he said. He couldn't see the boy, wanted a firm reassurance of his presence.

"I'm here."

"Well come over here by me. You have to stay close to me now. It's going to be snowing like hell soon and you don't want to get lost on me in the dark." They were ready to start. Granger eased the stitch in his back by stretching. "Let's have a look at that compass," he said. He tried to wipe his hands off before he got his cigarettes out. "Give me the compass," he said.

"I haven't got it."

"What? I said give it to me."

"I don't have it. I looked for it but I—" the boy started to say, but Granger was next to him, grabbed his wrist, wanting to shake him for not simply rolling up his sleeve and unbuckling the damn compass. He took his son's other hand.

"What the hell did you do with it?" He wasn't frightened, only puzzled. How could a boy lose a compass strapped to his wrist? "Did you put it in your pocket? Did you take it off somewhere? What the goddamn hell is wrong with you? Where is it?"

It wasn't in the boy's pockets. Granger lit matches and they searched the snow around the carcass. There was a moment in which Granger tore about in circles on his hands and knees, not hearing his son's weeping, and then he was standing, exhausted, looking into the blackness of the forest, hearing nothing more than the broken sound of his own breathing, feeling only the numbness in his hands and feet, the cold where the snow had melted, soaked through his clothing. Then he remembered that the older boys would wonder where in the hell they were. He found the rope tied to the deer carcass, but stopped, realizing he couldn't drag the deer; he didn't know the direction. There was no place to drag it to.

"Are we lost?" his son said.

"Lost? What the goddamn hell do you think we are? You throw the compass away, we're clear to hell back in hell's half acre, we're lost. I can't drag the deer in, we can't even move, see?" He was pleading as much for understanding, to make the boy see the enormity of his offense. "How do you ever expect to be able to go hunting when you're old enough? What's the matter with you, son, are you walking around in a daze? Don't you stay awake?"

"I'm sorry," the boy said. "I didn't mean to lose it. I don't remember if I took it off someplace or not."

Granger smoked another cigarette. Then they heard the three shots, hunter's distress signal, and he knew someone was looking for them. He found the rifle after a moment of panic when he couldn't remember where in relation to the carcass he'd put it, and fired three shots in the air. He didn't speak again to his son. There was another exchange of shots, then he heard the noise of someone coming fast through the brush and windfall, a voice calling his name. Smythe found them.

"Your boys come down and got me, Mr. Granger, just before I set off to get those does I shot today. How the hell'd you get lost in here?"

"We lost our compass," he said. That paid off the debt for the boy's lie about the squirrel. He was too tired to drag his deer, so Smythe put it across his shoulders and led them out.

In the cabin he had whiskey and sat close to the stove to thaw out. Al got the boy undressed, warmed, in bed.

Granger sat quietly, sipped the half-cup of whiskey straight. He took what Phil said. He wrote it off, the way a businessman writes off a tax loss, the years, the memories, the touch of hands and lips, the look and feel of trust. It was over, a bad debt, bad life. Let it go, Granger thought.

"You could have sent him down the road to the cabin," Phil said. "You should have better judgment. Mother won't hear about this because I'll see to it she won't, but it would create holy hell if she did. You of all people should know how she feels about his being with you. Maybe you don't like the way I'm talking to you, but I think it should be said. It doesn't matter with Allen and me because we know all we need to know. Mack's different. He doesn't know anything. What were you thinking of there when you took him with you after that deer, Dad? Do you *want* Mom to have an excuse to start poisoning him against you?"

"I'm sorry," Granger said, because he had to say something.

"It's just as well we're going home in the morning."

When he finished his whiskey he went to bed. He thought it was over, but it wasn't. During the night he had a pleasant surprise. He woke suddenly to find it cold, the tip of his nose feeling frosted, his hands hugged to his body. The arc of heat normally thrown by the oil-drum stove the Indian had made for him had shrunk, the fire subsided to the muffled fall of dying ashes. Next to him his youngest son was in a fetal curl, perhaps dreaming, Granger thought, of freezing to death while he wandered lost in the woods with his father.

Granger held his breath, tensed himself for the plunge into the icy air before he threw back the quilt to get up. He rose slowly from the bunk bed to avoid getting a crack on the head against the upper bunk. The moment his bare feet touched the wooden floor of the cabin, chills climbed his legs, making him unsteady, and the heavy cold settling into the shack seeped quickly through his woolen long-johns to his skin.

Quickly, careful to be quiet and not disturb the older boys, he crossed the room to the stove. He cursed the woodenness in his fingers, the helpless, steely-numb deadness that soaked into his feet. He shook down the dead ashes in the grate, dug a hole with the poker in the small lump of live coals remaining, then filled it with fresh briquets from the bag next to the stove. He closed the stove door, set the draft, hurried back to the bunk bed.

His son slid across the bed in his sleep, pressed himself fully up against his father's body for warmth. Granger lay still, felt his son instinctively adjust his head to his father's shoulder. The boy's feet, cold as nails, set themselves against Granger's legs. The boy whispered something inaudible and comfortable in his sleep, and then lay still against his father.

Granger passed one arm under the boy to form a cradle for him, thinking the boy was thirteen, too old to snuggle like a child. He held himself that way for a long time, until his circulation was obstructed and his arm and hand tingled, throbbed, went numb.

But he held himself that way for a long time because now he was close, touching the boy, and it didn't matter that the boy was asleep, because he was close and touching him, and he told himself he'd stay that way all night until the Big Ben alarm rang. The boy would wake, he told himself, see how his father touched him, held him. He would know it, and it would be enough no matter what he ever learned about his father—it would still be enough.

The others were too old, knew too much, couldn't trust and believe, but his youngest he touched, held, would sacrifice a night's sleep for, an arm if need be, to touch and hold. The hunt was a bust, but now in the night they were close.

His eyes burned and he swallowed with a loud click in his throat to keep from coughing. Though he told himself he'd stay awake that way all night, he fell asleep at last, and in the morning each was on his own side of the bunk. He told himself then it wasn't his fault he'd failed, he'd try again; the boy was young, knew nothing, didn't really ever have to learn, did he? But the hunt was over and everyone had to go home.

The boy's eyes opened and he said, "Is it morning?"

"Come on, it's time to get ready to go home, boy," Granger said.

He saw them off in their old Plymouth. After Granger tied the deer carcass on, his Chrysler wouldn't start; he had to hike down the road to the Indian's, get him to come and give him a push with the jeep.

All the way back to Minneapolis on the slippery roads he wondered how many chances he'd get before he died. Could there ever be enough future to pay for the past? The only answers he heard were the echoes of his own questioning voice.

The Two Sides of Things

"Don't continually say *hit me*." My Uncle Adolph spoke clearly without taking his black-and-silver cigarette holder from between his teeth. "It irritates the dealer," he said—he meant that it irritated him. "All you need do is scrape the edge of the table like this," he said, rasping the dining room table's felt pad with the edges of the deck of cards, as though he were sweeping crumbs toward his lap. "The dealer knows that way you want another card, and you don't have to irritate people by saying the same thing all the time. Now," he said, "try it." I scraped with the card in my hand. "Good," my uncle said. "Now let's get on with the game." He waited, one eyebrow raised, for me to call for yet another card.

With the five of clubs in my hand, it made eighteen. He had a jack showing. "I'm good," I said; I knew better than to say something like *I think I have all I want*. "I'm good," I repeated, wanting to be sure he noticed I remembered the correct words.

"I heard you the first time," he said, and, "Dealer pays twenty-one," said with confidence as he flipped over his blind card, a king. I swallowed my disappointment and pushed my cards over to him. He clenched his teeth, making the cigarette holder jut erectly up from his mouth, as he added to his score on the pinochle tablet he kept just to his right on the dining room table. It made him look a little like a thin President Roosevelt, in the famous photograph with his pince-nez and cigarette holder.

I remember my uncle marking the score with a ballpoint pen, a fairly new product then—it was 1948, and Uncle Adolph was convinced they would not last on the market. I was eleven, so never dreamed of second-guessing him. He was drubbing me unmercifully. He kept score in dollars, blackjack at a dollar a hand, casino at a dime a point; he said it was more interesting that way.

"You're forty bucks in the hole," he said to me. "In Vegas that's small change for the one-arm bandits. You couldn't get your hands on the dice with a roll no bigger than that." I nodded, seeing my Aunt Osa look up to smile very tolerantly at her husband's back. She sat at her escritoire, visible to me over my uncle's shoulder, on those evenings we played cards. Either she read, translating with moving lips, in an inaudible interior whisper, the Spanish of *Don Quixote de la Mancha*, or worked at her correspondence with the authors of cook books all over the world. The Spanish Club of Waukegan, Illinois, and the art of cooking: these were her world.

And that is the capsule, the essence of my memory of them: Uncle Adolph, inserting a fresh Sano into his filter-holder (it carried a cartridge, filled with crystals which blackened, signaling time for a change of filter), shuffling the cards while he eyed me through the smoke wreathing his head, like a Vegas sharper about to take a fat pigeon fresh from Cedar Rapids with the egg money burning a hole in his bib overalls; Aunt Osa, quietly prevailing in a spotless domestic comfort richened by elaborate menus and the time-resistant excellence of Cervantes.

My aunt's watchful control was, of course, smothering to me then, and my uncle's shameless crowing over cards was galling, but when I came to stay with them there in Waukegan, which was frequently during the year my father died of a liver disorder, I think I became a real person, in my sense of the word, for the first time in my life. That in itself makes them worth remembering, makes them worth cherishing in memory—I was only eleven, and it might have been less pleasant.

Because there was chaos and crisis at home, in Gary, Indiana, because of my father's alcoholism (aquavit is especially destructive of the liver), my mother sent me away often that last year . . . to give me a more *homey* atmosphere, as she would have put it. My other aunts, Anna and Claire, lived in Chicago, but they were less suitable, both being divorced. Aunt Claire had lived alone in Chicago since the twenties, when she cut something of a figure there after arriving from the family homestead, downstate in Hambro, Illinois, a farm town settled almost exclusively by Swedes.

I suppose the era was too exciting for my Aunt Claire's marriage to last. Her husband had something to do with bootlegging, and she would admit, if I persisted, that a fellow she went about with for a time ended up face down on the floor of a garage on a particular St. Valentine's Day.

Aunt Anna's husband, my Uncle Knute, had become wealthy during the second war, selling a part of a machine that made a part of a machine that made something useful in war. They were divorced when he took up with a woman he met in Minneapolis on a business trip. Aunt Anna's divorce was too recent, in 1948, for my mother to foist me on her. So I was sent to Aunt Osa's and Uncle Adolph's.

I was attracted to my uncle to begin with. For one thing, he detested my name—I was given Bengt, after my father and Grandfather Berntsson both—as much as I did. I cannot recall him ever using it to speak to me. For another, he was not comfortable talking to his wife or her sisters, or my father (who was almost always inebriated), so he talked to me when we got together as a family. This is a novelty with some charm, when you are only eleven.

On the occasions we gathered, in Gary or Chicago, for birthdays, Christmas, and Thanksgiving, I was lost below the level of adults who recollected childhood days in Hambro, ate huge meals of (to me) unappetizing Swedish food, and drank aquavit with beer chasers, my aunts staying drink for drink with my father. In short, I was lonely; my aunts were all childless.

"Who's your favorite baseball player?" Uncle Adolph asked me, peering over the edge of the sports page. My father, for example, would never have thought to ask.

"Jackie Robinson," I said without thinking, merely eager to give an answer when someone had somehow taken the trouble to care if I had one. Uncle Adolph cared indeed, frowning severely at my reply. I had answered too quickly, forgetting his background, as told to me by my mother and my aunts.

"What kind of an answer is that?" he said. "My God, is there any reason you can't have a white man for your favorite, boy?" He snapped the newspaper together and folded it against his chest. "What's the matter with Ewell Blackwell? Now there's a man to be your favorite. What's wrong with Ralph Branca if it has to be a Dodger?"

He could always intimidate me. I weakly mumbled that it did not have to be a Dodger—I thought a lot of Blackwell, and Branca, and Dixie Walker too. At least we could agree that there was no use in caring for the limping Cubs or White Sox, either one.

My Uncle Adolph was born and raised in Memphis, and this part of him had not been exorcised by his travels. He was touchy about it, denying prejudice if my mother challenged him on it. He would respond with the story of betting on Jack Johnson against Stan Ketchel, which was, he smugly asserted, hardly the wager of a prejudiced man.

And he had traveled. He joined the navy in 1908 (an impossibly prehistoric date to me!), and prior to that had logged some time on merchant ships. I loved the stories he told, of course.

What I love about them now is that he told them with the idea, I think, of suggesting something special, something hideous, for example, that could not be spoken plainly of in front of women. Aunt Osa used to contend jokingly that she had civilized him, for all the Old South and its culture, by accepting his proposal there in Hambro, Illinois, when he showed up at the end of his travels to operate the telegraph for the Illinois Central Railroad, in 1916. These impulses, his and hers, are at the center of my *person*, my being a person at about age eleven, in 1948.

There was, for instance, the story of his shipwreck off the Borneo coast.

"The damn ship rolled over on her side like a foundered horse. The suction must have taken the others down with her. I made the half-mile in from the reef, not knowing yet I was one of two survivors—" he said before I broke in. We were playing casino this time, and I was, as usual, losing heavily.

"Who was the other one?"

"Galley slavey," he said, "cook's helper—boy, don't interrupt me that way!" He had some sense that my mother's sending me to stay for a few weeks involved his responsibility to teach me some masculine social manners. I did not mind; it implied my importance, that I must be worth the effort it cost him, that I was considered a potential gentleman, requiring such manners.

"It's *very* impolite to break into a man's story, boy! What's more, what did you forget?" He waited, grim behind the smoke of his Sano cigarette, while I tried hard to concentrate.

"*Sir?*"

"That's right. *Sir.* Show others respect and they'll respect you," he said. "You can walk with kings, and they'll respect you." He said this with a change in the expression around his eyes that tempted me to look behind me and see whether or not some royal entourage had, in fact, joined us from the kitchen to validate my uncle's proposition. What it expressed was the poignancy of his disappointment at never having walked with them himself—because he felt, I think, that they, those anonymous kings, *would* have respected him. In shaping my deportment he was treating his own sense of failure in life.

I recall this statement whenever I read the blurb saying horse racing is the sport of kings. Uncle Adolph also played the horses. After the fashion, that is, that his wife permitted. He subscribed to *Racing Form* and a couple of Chicago tout sheets; he concentrated on the season at Washington Park, recorded his bets, and the results, all without risking a single dollar. It was like our card games, all a controlled exercise of his pure fancy.

I have seen him sit close to my father on their visits to Gary, pushing his recorded bets between my father and the aquavit jug, pointing with the trembling tip of his mechanical pencil, showing my father how he was making a killing, killing upon killing, on the ponies.

"Look here," Uncle Adolph said, "three hundred this week, three seventy-five, three twenty, and this . . . this was a bad week, just over a hundred. A hundred is a *bad* week for me. Now repeat to me I'm dreaming. Right here in black and white. . . ." Maybe he was trying to persuade my father to stake him for a real crack at the horses with his system, for Uncle Adolph, who pushed a pencil in the production control department for U.S. Steel in Waukegan, could not afford to bet much, and my Aunt Osa would not allow him to bet anything.

What he dreamed of was just exactly the kind of fast and fat win the horseplayer and gambler enjoy. And I believe he wanted me to know this. I believe it was important to my Uncle Adolph that I should perceive, and should respect, this flash of colorful, exciting dream-wish that lay buried beneath his steady, reliable, dull and aging exterior. The proper manners, he said, enabled you to walk with the kings of the earth . . . and I was meant to understand that he, at least, was up to it, at least in imaginative achievements, no matter how utterly absurd this all was against the realities of his life.

"As I was saying before you interrupted. I didn't know until morning that there was another survivor besides myself. We met on the beach in the first light of day after our ship went down on that reef." He paused, as if bracing himself to deal with another interruption, but I kept silence, and, over his shoulder, my aunt's lips moved soundlessly over her Spanish.

"We began to cut our way through the jungle, because we knew that it couldn't be too far to some civilization. The Dutch had naval installations in the area, but we'd heard that the locals sometimes took a man's head for a trophy without first asking his permission. We were ill-equipped. I had a revolver, a big single-action smoker— which I always carried on my person in those days—and my partner had a butcher knife, which he'd had sense enough to grab in the galley before he hopped over the ship's rail.

"We had been going about a day and a half. I heard him scream out behind me—I was breaking trail at the time—" Here he stopped quite unashamed, for dramatic effect, and also, possibly, tempting me, to see if I had taken the lesson about interrupting to heart. He liked to do that, test my self-control. At blackjack, when he knew I was praying for a low card, a deuce or tray at most, in order to come in under twenty-one with five cards, and so chip two dollars off my mounting losings, he would delay the flip of the fifth card off the top of the deck. Testing me. But I could do it if I tried.

"He screamed," he went on, "and I turned around with my pistol already on cock, but it was too late. Some breed of boa constrictor had dropped around his neck from the limb of a tree. He was dead before I could shoot. It happened that fast."

"Really? Sir?" I asked. He was too sensitive, and not so cruel, as to construe that I suspected the whole tale to be so much malarkey; he understood that I merely wanted its emotional reality confirmed, a last time, by the man before me, who was the very horse's mouth. It allowed him, too, the opportunity to plant the suggestion that is the crux, or his half of it, of the sense of *person*, of being, of oneself, of identity in time and place, that was his real gift to me.

"That's what I told the proper authorities, in any case," he said, leaning back in the dining room chair, the suggestion of the too-hideous in his eyes, the flash of his teeth clamped down on his cigarette filter-holder as he leered at me, his hand seeming to reach out, unwilled, to give the deck of cards a one-handed sharper's cut. Oh, he succeeded!

Sometimes, in the right mood, I still reserve the right to think it *was* pure malarkey, that my uncle made it up out of whole cloth, simply to impress and delight me. But again, at other times, in other moods, I need—*need*—to believe there was something too terrible to give utterance. Might they not have argued over cards, for instance? Certain it is that my Uncle Adolph admired those who did it and got away with it, even if only for a short time.

I have heard him speak of the Chicago gangster who dated my Aunt Claire, the one killed on St. Valentine's Day. Uncle Adolph spoke of him, of his fashionable clothes, his fast car, the lump in his coat where his pistol rested, in a tone that made it clear he would have approved an alliance with that outlaw. He and Aunt Osa had rented a flat in Cicero for a time back then, and Uncle Adolph recalled the violence of bootlegging days fondly.

He had me stand up, there in the parlor in Waukegan, had me put out my hand to shake with him; I was acting the role of Deeny O'Banion, while my uncle was the uncaught gunsel sent to make the hit—my uncle had several theories about just how the gun was concealed in the killer's hand until the instant he raised it to fire.

Uncle Adolph held that, morally, John Dillinger was more respectable than either the woman in red who fingered him, or the FBI agents who shot him down in front of the Biograph.

"Granted he was a thief and a murderer," my uncle said, "there was nothing wishy-washy about him. Good Indiana farmboy stock to begin with. Someday we'll have to drive over to Crown Point and see the grave where they say they buried what was left of him." I was eleven, and it was magnificent.

My Uncle Adolph disliked Jackie Robinson, because that was bred into him in Memphis. But he knew better than to bet on Stan Ketchel, and he admired Satchel Paige for holding onto his arm long past retirement age for ordinary men. Nigger or not, old Satchel was still getting away with it! He thought the Black Sox were simply dumb, because they got caught so quickly and easily, and Shoeless Joe Jackson the dumbest of the lot, because, unlike Eddie Cicotte and the others, he got no money out of it.

His all-time favorite baseball player was a man named Snodgrass, who had played third base, years before, for John McGraw's Giants. "He played third," my uncle said, "and he was something to wonder at. When a man was on third, waiting to tag up and go to beat the throw home on a long fly ball, this Snodgrass I'm telling you about would slip two fingers under the man's belt, pretending to play close to the bag. Snodgrass would hold him up, just for a split second, enough to keep him from making it to the plate ahead of the throw. They had a center fielder, I forget his name, with an arm like a rifle. He did it for more than a year. Nobody knew how long he got away with it but Snodgrass himself, I imagine. They finally caught him out." That was the way of the world, my uncle's voice implied; everyone always got caught out in the end, even Al Capone, and it was worse than unfair; it was tragic.

"Some wiseacre thought to remove the buckle from his belt before he went up to hit. He got to third, there was a fly ball, he tagged up and took off, and there was Snodgrass with the ump and both teams and a park full of fans watching him, standing over the bag with the runner's belt in his hand."

Uncle Adolph looked away while lighting a fresh Sano; we grieved, both of us, for Snodgrass, and for the fact that nobody ever gets away with it in the end, ever.

It has to do with secrets. I learned that men have secrets that cannot bear telling—witness the forever uncertain demise of the cook's helper in the wilds of Borneo. I learned men have secret desires—for riches, for fast and fat triumphs that depend upon evil or inside information. Men want to walk with whoever passes for royalty in our country. I learned things are not what they seem, that behind my uncle's very ordinary facade lay elements unguessed by any except initiates to those secrets, like myself. What, for example, I began to wonder, waited inside my own alcoholic father's stony and indifferent exterior for me to uncover? What might lie, in time, within me?

It has nothing to do with finding out secrets. It is only that they exist to baffle and fascinate us. This I learned, and became something other than I had been, as I looked up to watch my Aunt Osa, preoccupied at her escritoire. And I knew I had learned it, which is yet another secret of being alive.

One has to learn there are secrets, and then one has to learn to live with them. My uncle came to this, this learning, when he met my Aunt Osa. He may have learned it already, but he came to accept it when he married her.

In 1916 he was thirty years old, and outside his navy-taught skill as a telegrapher, and the stories gathered in his travels, he had nothing to show for his life. On the contrary, when he landed the job with the Illinois Central and came to Hambro, he had been used rather badly. He was underweight and sickly from the experience of his last job, working the key out of a tiny relay station near Utica, Mississippi. My aunt, it seemed to me, could always find some excuse to tell her side of it.

The casino and twenty-one were over for the night, but my uncle kept on talking, and had gotten around to the general subjects of food and eating. I think he was telling me about the *frijoles refritos* he had eaten in Mexico once, the time he made a special trip across the border to meet and shake hands with Francisco Madero, who was encamped just south of Brownsville then. Uncle Adolph could not speak of food without bitterness, for he had had, a couple of years earlier, the ulcer operation that removed fourteen inches of his intestines. He evaded his rigid diet whenever he dared.

He said something like, "You take a gob of those beans on a *tortilla*, boy, and you dash some of that red sauce they grind up from peppers on a stone all over it, and then, by God, you stick the whole shebang right in your mouth. . . ."

My aunt looked up from *Don Quixote*. I prefer to think she understood every bit of what his stories meant to me. I prefer to think she understood, and so determined that I should see the other side of it —her side; the second of those two sides people always say exist about any question of import. She was being deliberately fair to me, not cruel to him.

She got up and came behind his chair. She put her hand on his shoulder, her wedding band prominent against the black of his unbuttoned vest. Although she pretended to be talking to him at first, her eyes never let go of mine.

"Oh," Aunt Osa said, "and why don't you tell him how much you liked goat meat." Uncle Adolph carefully placed another Sano in his filter-holder and lit it, turning off his attention, as though saying: I have heard all this before. This is for the boy, not me. I already know; I have already accepted.

"Adolph had a job relaying dispatches at some dinky little backwater station in Mississippi, just before he came to Hambro. The railroad paid a farmer and his wife to room and board him because it was the only house within miles of the station. The first morning there he found out what that was going to be like."

Uncle Adolph went *ungh*, once, but it may have only been the smoke in his throat choking him.

"He stepped out of bed," my aunt went on," straight smack dab with his bare foot in some goat dung." I giggled. "Yes! Right in the bedroom, and you could smell it all through the house! Goats in the house!" I think I laughed again, louder. My uncle shifted in his chair, pinned there by the gently resting weight of his wife's hand. She held me with her eyes.

"And how that woman fed him! Fried dough, just fried in a deep fat, and coffee with chicory in it, and very rarely some ham, because they kept pigs too. He nearly starved to death. He couldn't bring himself to complain, nor could he eat it.

"Then one day while he was working, one of the man's fool goats was killed by a train. Your uncle ran up to the house to tell him, and the farmer got his knife and ran down to the tracks and bled the goat and dressed it out. Well they ate goat. It was the first decent meat he'd had in so long, and of course they had no refrigeration, so there was goat, fried in deep fat, meal after meal." My uncle swallowed audibly, and closed his eyes, pulled steadily on the bit of his cigarette filter-holder.

"When that ran out," Aunt Osa said, "it was back to fried dough again—because naturally the man wasn't going to care what he fed Adolph; he got paid for room and board regardless. Now tell Bengt what you did then . . . when you couldn't stand any more fried dough."

My uncle looked at me, opened his eyes, discovering an expression I had not seen before. He carefully knocked the ash from the tip of his Sano against the glass lip of the ashtray before he spoke. As if to say: No matter how ridiculous, no matter how humiliating, this *is* the truth. Like Alphonse Capone's income taxes and syphilis, there comes, finally, to all men, that *truth* that defies our desires, no matter what the grandeur, the enormity, or even the triviality. Yes, I understood: we dream secrets, all of us . . . and they fail us, and we fail them. And we must live with that.

"I bided," Uncle Adolph said, as if he were reciting a piece committed to memory, "my time. Until I could be sure there was no one in sight. The farmhouse was over a rise, so it wasn't particularly difficult or long in coming. I enticed a goat down to my station shack, and tethered him there. Sometimes, later, I'd have it all planned, on a schedule, so as to have only a five- or ten-minute wait, me there holding the bleating goat by its horns. When the train came I'd shove the goat under the wheels and run for the house to tell the farmer. He'd get his knife."

"And they'd eat goat again," Aunt Osa said. "Goat meat fried in deep fat." She quaked at the thought of it. "And that," she said, "is what ruined your uncle's stomach." I knew that he had had a very rough time with the ulcer operation; he never really recovered his health again, though he was not to die for many years to come. "If he'd stayed there longer before coming to work in Hambro he'd like to have died long ago as a result," she said. And she meant that, literally. And he believed it too. She had made her point; she went back to Cervantes, and my uncle squinted through cigarette smoke as he shuffled the cards for a last game of casino before my bedtime.

Later, that same night, when she had left the room, he leaned close to me to whisper, "God though, boy," he said, "that old farm woman could make a goat taste like something!"

He did not tell his stories of Borneo or Mexico to provoke her, and she did not bring up his bachelor absurdities to retaliate. They merely recognized, each, their respective strengths. He could not survive without the flavor of foolish dreams, and she knew no one dared try to live except with respect for reality. This is what each sought to teach me.

My father's mother, Grandmother Berntsson, died giving birth to my father. Aunt Osa was nearly twenty then, and she shared the housekeeping with an old spinster woman named Sorenson, who had more or less tagged along on the journey from Sweden to Hambro, Illinois, with the Berntsson family. By the time Uncle Adolph arrived in Hambro, my Aunt Anna had married Uncle Knute and moved away. My father was an irretrievably spoiled child of ten; my aunts attributed his adult alcoholism, and his early death, to the indulgences he was permitted as a motherless boy. And by then, almost thirty years old, my Aunt Osa's prospects could hardly have seemed very favorable to her, especially in light of Aunt Claire's already showing signs of becoming too beautiful for a small town to contain. Claire was twenty by then, and Chicago was beckoning; Prohibition was only a few years away.

My Aunt Osa faced becoming an old maid, with a future to be lived out in the same house where she was born, with the care of Grandfather Berntsson and the spinster Sorenson to assume as they aged into senility.

Then my uncle came, knocked at the porch door to ask if he might take his meals with the Berntsson family, who lived near the railroad station; the Illinois Central paid, now, a per diem to spend, for that purpose, anywhere he pleased.

So it all ended rather happily, in a way. My father died of cirrhosis of the liver, but I was spared seeing much of that, because I was so often visiting my aunt and uncle. And in time, they died too.

Aunt Osa outlived him. The last time I saw him, they came to visit me and my wife, in Levittown, Pennsylvania, where I lived a few years ago. Uncle Adolph was, I think, about seventy-five then.

My wife and my aunt were getting up a little lunch in the kitchen —it was separated from the living room by a four-sided fireplace in a

Levitt house—and my uncle and I were watching baseball on television in the living room. I got up and said I'd go out to the shopping center for some beer.

"He's not supposed to drink beer, Bengt," my aunt stepped in from the kitchen to say.

"One little can won't hurt," I said. "We can't watch the game without beer." My uncle listened closely, finger pressing the earpiece of his hearing aid deeper into his ear. When it was clear she would not protest further, he got up and picked up his hat.

"I'll come along for the ride," he said. He had had his first stroke just about a year before. I knew it was the last trip east he would ever make; east or anywhere, it was the end of his travels, though I had no special premonition he would die before the year was out. I had to keep a firm grip on his thin, fragile arm as he walked to my car, for he refused to use his cane.

They had the ball game on TV at the small quickie bar in the shopping center, and Uncle Adolph suggested we get a beer while we were there, so as not to miss the Yankees' turn at bat. While he deprecated contemporary sports heroes—Mantle nor Mays, neither one, was a Ruth or a Rogers Hornsby, much less a Nap Lajoie or a Louie F. Sockalexis—still, he liked to watch someone with a good chance of hitting one out of the park. He attributed all the home runs to the rabbit ball; Frank Baker would have murdered the lively ball, my uncle said.

"Put a head on this for us," he said to the bartender when he had finished his glass. He made a great show of peeling a bill off his roll, tossing it on the bar to pay for our beer. He stood out at the bar, one spindly, pathetically thin leg up, pointed shoe on the rail, in the stance of a much younger man, one accustomed to bending his elbow for a couple of hours each day. My uncle scrutinized the chalkboard recording the baseball pool the bar ran with a professional eye; he could have told them a few things about odds. I had the silly notion that he was going to ask the bartender for the dice cup, then challenge me to roll for a shot of straight whiskey. But that was my imagination, not his.

Dressed in a suit with matching vest, the chain of his railroad watch looped across the slight bulge of his paunch, the authentic straw skimmer from his mature manhood of the twenties cocked on his head, he was like some piece of antique furniture in the chromed, paneled, tiled quickie bar. Or like a cutout, a figure removed from the photograph of a big-city saloon of forty years before, pasted in our midst, the whole a superficial ironist's collage. I could taste with my beer, smell with the smoke of the cigar he bought, peeled, pierced, and lit after sniffing, a sense of the dimension of time stronger than any I have known since.

He admitted the second glass of beer made him a little dizzy, so we went home with a six-pack.

After another beer, after lunch, after the game was over, he seemed to withdraw into himself. I suggested we play a little cards, blackjack or casino. Through college, the army, my married life, I had played no cards, but I wanted, for some reason, to get him talking to me. He won the deal on the cut.

"No," he said, breaking his silence as he dealt the hands, "you've done nicely for yourself, boy. Yes," he said, "you've got a job that you can be respected for doing well, you've got a lovely wife—your aunt and I think a great deal of the girl you married. You've got every right to look the world in the eye . . . to be respected." I do not know how he happened to hit on exactly what I wanted; I could not have said, then, that I knew that was what I wanted so badly to hear. It is the kind of thing that comes to all of us, I hope.

There are the moments when we suddenly feel we have failed ourselves, have betrayed or frittered away what was once best in us, when even our ambitions seem to have evaporated into a filmy mess, when only sour memories come to us when we call on the past for help. They are nothing, these moments, for a man to dwell upon, but they will come.

This moment passed for me, in my uncle's kind words, and then we played some blackjack. I decided to risk another card, the fifth, with fourteen. I scratched my hand on the table top, but he did not lay out my fifth card. "Hit me again," I said, looking up from my cards.

"Shhh," my aunt said softly, coming from the kitchen and taking the deck out of his hands. "He's dozed off from all that beer you gave him. He usually takes a nap in the afternoon at home."

I sat back in my chair and watched him, sleeping. From time to time there was a flutter under his eyelids, a twitch at one corner of his mouth, the way there is when a sleeping man is dreaming.

I Go Back

In Chicago, if you are not fortunate enough to live near the lake-front, August is intolerable. So is having nothing to do. So I went back this past summer.

I had finished my dissertation ("Joseph Conrad: The Juxtaposition of Reality and Vision") at the University of Illinois in early July, before the summer sun had settled down seriously to bake the Champaign-Urbana prairie and make the corn grow. With the aid of my major professor in the English department I obtained an assistant professorship at a small denominational college in Vermont. I was not scheduled to arrive there until the end of August.

"It's strictly bush league, Allen," my professor said, dramatically sad, "but you've got to remember it's late to be angling for an appointment, so we can't be choosers, can we?" We could not.

My wife, Lynne, was tired of typing invoices and license plate applications for a local automobile agency that stayed one precarious step ahead of the law. I was tired, respectfully so, of Conrad. And it only stood to reason that my wife's parents were at least receptive to the prospect of my repaying the money they had loaned me to allow me to concentrate on Conrad. I was ready to begin the great adventure of earning a living. The sooner the better for all concerned.

There was not time to visit my in-law creditors in Oregon; they were invited to spend Christmas in Vermont. We packed together the surprising bulk of books, odd pieces of secondhand furniture, and malfunctioning household appliances for our trip with rented trailer to Chicago, where my mother had kindly invited us to exist parasitically until the departure east was imminent.

I shook dry hands with a half-score of professors who tried to recall just who *I* was in their galleries of former students. We scraped together the money to buy a pony of Edelweiss beer, and in our third-story apartment, shorn of the cheap reprints on the walls, all three rooms bare, we held a last party for fellow graduate students and their wives (in one case, a husband: he painted; she was preparing for her preliminary examinations and discussed the feasibility of Mark Twain's "Desperate Naturalism" as a dissertation problem.)

Perhaps it began at the party. We sat on the floors and leaned against the sloping walls, smoking too much, drinking Edelweiss from paper cups, keeping an eye open for a moment when the bathroom would be free, and talked shop, which is fashionable in graduate circles. For it is one great workshop—no one *does* anything in graduate school, one only meticulously *prepares* to do in the indefinite future. We played literary games ("I'm W. B. and I wrote poetry." "Did you also do engraving?" "No, I'm not William Blake."), which are also permissible.

I think it began at the party. We all looked alike: the women plain for the most part, a few more maternal than the others, a few relatively attractive; the men all wearing suit jackets without ties. Sweaters predominated. No one was under twenty-seven, no one older than thirty-six (one old bachelor). We shared facial techniques for expressions of bored sophistication, scholarly impatience, and watered-down academic idealism. In time, I saw, we would fan out (the occasion was *my* fanning out) and eagerly people the faculty rolls of colleges and universities, Ivy League, West Coast, big league, and (like me) bush league.

After which we would dustily set ourselves to the teaching of classes, the reading of books, and for the ambitious, the mobile, the writing of learned papers. In time, I saw we would shake dry hands with graduating students we had known, but *who*, exactly, we would not remember. I detected purpose in my vision, yes, but a vague one, seen grayly, a collage of minuscule bits and pieces. Whence the significance?

My wife was seated on the arm of an unstable wooden chair, talk-

ing with the painter fellow. My eye caught him, moustached, beard-
ed, unkempt to a fault, squeezing a scorching cigarette end between
two fingertips. "I still don't see how you can say that," Lynne said.
"Who are you to simply deny the competence of the *entire* U. of I.
art faculty?" His eyeballs moved wickedly upward in their sockets.

That's all well and good for you, I thought at him, *you're not tied
up in this mess*. For, at most, the tenth part of a second, I wished to
take Lynne's hand and lead her down the two flights of steep steps
into the street below. I wanted to take her with me in my retreat, my
escape—but to go, and quickly.

Because she continued expostulating with the painter, who smugly
provoked her and thought himself smart with carping cracks at the
art department, I knew an even shorter time of selfish willingness to
abandon her and run alone, only run. Of course this all passed.

So when I decided to go, in mid-August, for a weekend with Lynne
to my mother's summer cottage in Wisconsin where I had spent my
summers until I was in high school, it is possible I was not *going* anywhere then, but rather was running further still from my brief and
bleak vision. My mother didn't like it.

"You can't go up there, Allen," she said. "It hasn't been opened
up for the summer. You only have another week before you have to
leave."

"It's only for a weekend," I said, "and Lynne's never had a chance
to see it. There's always been summer school or a paper or something in the way. Now there isn't. We'll be back in a couple of days at
most."

"Go then if you think you have to," my mother said.

"Maybe we shouldn't," Lynne said.

"I think we should."

The trip was easily done; that was the big difference. As a boy, the
trip was a long journey to a foreign country. Lynne and I talked a
good part of the way and listened to the radio in the faithful hoarse
Hudson we'd owned for three years (fifth-hand when purchased).
There was not even time to feel hungry. We stopped out of concern
for our roaring Hudson at a gleaming sanitary gas-station coffee-
shop on Highway 41 between Fond du Lac and Oshkosh. The
names: *Fond du Lac, Oshkosh*—different sounding, surprisingly,

delightfully new and more real.

"Fond du Lac," I explained to Lynne, "is French."

"Thank you so much, Doctor," she said.

"No negative thinking now. It means, not the bottom of the lake, in the sense of the floor of the lake, but the bottom end of Lake Winnebago in the sense of north: top, south: bottom." *Winnebago*: again the name. To say it makes me hope an Indian will walk into my classroom in Vermont, reeking of dirty blanket, fresh-killed game, and natural nobility. Say it silently in the clean restroom of a Howard Johnson's: it causes laughter, deeply inside.

"Oshkosh," I told Lynne, "was the last chief to hold the power of life and death over his people, the Menominee. He lived well into the middle of the nineteenth century." I had met his granddaughter when a high school friend of mine married his great-granddaughter.

"Shall I take notes?"

"That's negative. Chief Oshkosh's people no longer live here, but to the north, around Shawano and Neopit—" the names—"and the city at the northern end of Lake Winnebago named for him is today famous for overalls and, in a minor way, beer, which proves how strange are the means by which a man's name may live on after him."

"So noted," Lynne said.

But before I exhausted that tone, we were there. The difference: my trips north as a boy were epic in a contemporary fashion. Lynne and I merely drove, the Hudson bellowed through the rent in its exhaust pipe, and the radio played—stations began to advertise Purina stock feeds, lime and phosphates for the health of the soil—and we arrived. And I arrived with my eyes spinning with all that was supposed to but had not happened on the trip.

When my mother drove us to the cottage for those summers, there were two moods to observe. One was for calculated entertainment. She drove, both hands on the wheel of our '41 Plymouth, the speedometer needle locked precisely on 45 miles per hour, her back straight, eyes trying to penetrate the dancing light on the horizon, perched high on a cushion so she could see the fenders, and I entertained. I knew she listened though her eyes never wavered, her head never cocked or canted.

I could imitate instruments. By humming and pulling on my nose I did a nasal electric guitar playing "Beautiful Hawaii." The sensitive tip of my nose would not permit me to sustain the tempo of war chants for long. The tuba was easy, a bit beneath me. I did a Jew's harp and sang the chorus, "My Ma don't 'low no Jew's harp 'round this house." This led into my singing.

My tour de force was Wee Bonnie Baker. And though I knew my mother wouldn't let me finish, I always started the "Whiffenpoof Song" in Louis Armstrong's gravel voice.

"Stop that, Allen," she said.

"Why? It sounds just like him and you know it does. Why shouldn't I?"

"Because it makes my teeth jangle to hear it. If you keep that up it'll ruin your throat. How would you like to always have to talk that way?"

Then she would mention Baxter, the postman who delivered our mail at the cottage and who took me along on his rural route if I got up early enough to meet his government Chevrolet at our mailbox. He swallowed mustard gas in the trenches during the first war. His voice was a raw rasp, and because he persisted in leaving a Camel in his mouth while he leaned across me in the front seat to reach out the window and put the letters in the boxes, he suffered long fits of choking that shook him until he seized his chest with both hands for composure.

My mother never permitted me to cross my eyes either; they might stick that way, and then what would I do?

I did radio personalities (no radio in our Plymouth). In falsetto, Fred Allen's Portland was shrill but recognizable. I liked "Allen's Alley." About the time I reached Senator Claghorn's door, my mother had had enough.

"Ah say, boy, Ah say, boy, listen to me now, boy," I said with appropriate congressional gestures, which were what probably decided her.

"That's enough now," she said.

"What's wrong? What's the matter? It sounds just like him." Her teeth were set firm, and she began to lean toward the steering wheel, squinting. If I kept protesting she would be sure to curse an innocent motorist coming in the opposite direction for hogging the road, or verbally abuse farmers who had the gall to block the highway (this was *old* 41, two lanes of blacktop only) with tractors and hayracks.

I had my cue to be silent. I was reduced to counting telephone poles and cows, identifying the makes and models of passing cars, and being careful to make no outcry if a pheasant exploded at the side of the road, or I saw a hawk hovering above us, or men at work on the land looked up to see us go by.

Quiet and tense, we inched our path north to Oshkosh, from there west to Silver Lake, at no more nor less than the rate of 45 miles per hour.

There was an institutional stop to be made. Unlike my wife and I (I got a steady 65-70 mph out of the commodious Hudson), my mother and I did get hungry.

At Omro (not an Indian name, but still one with potential) we always stopped at a place called Lana and Wally's. She was the only Lana in the world besides Turner, thus impressive. Lana had red hair I know now was hennaed, and she always served us tepid water in marred pink translucent plastic tumblers before handing us menus. Wally her husband had a receding hairline, a cleft chin, a paunch pulled drum-taut by an apron, a tattoo (butterfly, left forearm), and a conspicuous hearing aid.

He fried me a hamburger, thin and flat at first, that expanded its middle and contracted its edges. The bun was set on the greasy griddle to warm slightly, and one disk of papery dill pickle accompanied it on the small plate. Their malteds were frothy and thin, made with malt powder scooped from a Horlick's container. Lana pursed her lips and was generous with the ice cream on my pumpkin pie, her arms quivering, tendons hard, as she dug deeply in the pit of the ice cream freezer.

My mother ate a chicken salad sandwich with black coffee, frugal fare to me, but perhaps her nerves required discipline where mine needed to be glutted. She always had exact change for Lana, who totaled the bill on a green pad carried clipped to her waist, her lips moving as she did addition.

Wally, if there were no other customers to cook for, rested against the joint of counter and wall, under the face of Chief Oshkosh advertising his beer, and fiddled with the dial on his hearing aid. After gasoline and an oil check we continued on our way. The second war was on, and our Plymouth bore a C sticker in the lower right corner of the windshield.

"Won't it be nice to just drive in and say 'fill it up' again?" my mother often asked gas station attendants. Old men, boys, and 4-F's, a few agreed, some muttered, and others were noncommittal.

We drove past Lana and Wally's at a legal 25 miles per hour. Omro has added a sleek, lethal, gray-green pursuit squad that carries out the posted threat of radar, manned by an anonymous trooper who wears sunglasses.

I was sorry at first that we did not stop. Now I see I was wise. I told Lynne about the restaurant, but had we gone in, Lana and Wally would not have been as I described them, both because I do not describe accurately (one remembers little; the rest must be made up) and because they would have been different. Lana's pride may have diminished, her hair allowed to go naturally gray or white. Perhaps Wally's deafness has progressed and he sits in a noiseless corner, watching his trade. Worse, one of them might be dead, and my memory so made unreal. We reached Silver Lake all too soon.

There were so many things that I had not had time enough to miss seeing. The drive was so smooth and quick, no broken fanbelts or flat tires or boiling radiators to make our destination the more desirable by threatening to keep us from it. I chatted too easily with my wife and listened too conscientiously to the silliness of the radio to notice enough changes. But by telling Lynne of the strangeness of what I saw then, I was made aware of what I had seen twenty years before, and by failing to find what I had once found, I was forced to look within myself for it.

So my flight from the minute and the complicating and the indefinable became a search for the large, the particular, the things with names.

"I'm going to lie on the beach on a blanket and get an even tan," Lynne said.

Library-white, I said, "Not me, I'm going to move around. I wonder if two days will be enough?" And of course it was, and it was not.

West from Oshkosh on Highway 21, after passing through Omro, bypassing Berlin (during the war the citizen patriots altered the pronunciation of the name), there was only the town of Redgranite between us and Silver Lake. The quarry that paved many of the nation's streets is defunct and water-filled now, and were it not for the pickle cannery that has brought employment to Redgranite in recent years, it would be a ghost town. After Redgranite, the first local landmark lies on the left heading west.

The Woodcraft Camp for Boys, now affiliated with the Reformed Lutheran Church, employed me for a time during my thirteenth summer.

"That's where I worked once," I told Lynne. The authentic Alaskan totem pole, its faces faded and cracked, still sentinels the gate. Next to it there is a sign with a Christian cross and the name of the new owners.

"Oh," she said, "when you were the stableboy? That time?"

"Let's just call me a ranchhand." Neither is correct. Only the counselor, a man studying veterinary medicine on the G.I. Bill at the University of Wisconsin, wore cowboy boots and hat. I did shovel troughs and hay the stock, but it was more, of more moment than that. I sat on the cool stone floor of the hay barn and soaped saddles until my palms puffed smoothly and the skin around my fingernails wrinkled. I rubbed neat's-foot oil into bridles and halters until my food smelled of it. But more.

When the paying campers my age wandered down to the barn during free periods, released from beadcraft, bow-making, and swimming lessons, I picked up currying comb and brush and walked calmly into the stall of a tethered buckskin horse noted for biting and kicking. I slapped its rump half-hard, pushed it to one side of the stall, and growled *Hiya!* at the beast as if I myself might bite or kick if resisted.

While the campers, crispy in stenciled tee shirts and red short pants, leaned against the front of the stall, pretending not to notice me, I combed or curried or cleaned, chucking now and then to the buckskin, terrified by its rolling eye whites and flattened ears, the clump of its shod feet making me squeeze my toes together inside my canvas shoes, but intoxicated almost to the point of sweet-sour nausea by my own sense of self-importance, as it came to me, mixed with the rich smell of feed and stall bedding, or was conveyed to my hand by the touch of a quivering flank or the wiry texture of a tangled mane.

"Did they pay you for that?" my wife asked me. She had no intention of deflating my memory, and really, she did not.

"I got to ride all day on Sundays," I said. "Otherwise people from outside the camp had to pay four bits an hour. I rode free."

"Was that *before* child labor legislation?"

"Cut it out. Here we are." We had reached the Moose, a tavern on the right side of the highway, marking the left turn that led to my mother's cottage on the lake. I insisted we have a drink despite the early afternoon hour.

"Is that relic real?" Lynne asked.

"Certainly. It's just been dead for fifty or sixty years. You'll be lucky if you look so good then." That much had not changed. It is a good, conventional, respectable-looking moose's head from a short distance. When I walked under it to enter the tavern, I saw that the eyeballs were painted glass, the nostrils had been plugged with putty, and hornets had essayed a nest on one rack of its horns. Weathering has made the hide like dark brown sailcloth, and overall there were the bodies of gnats and mosquitoes, wrapped individually by the spider that strung its hairy net like a shabby veil over the animal's face.

"I don't believe it's real," Lynne said.

"I do."

Originally (meaning when I first came to the area with my mother —time begins with me) the tavern was owned by a man and his wife, referred to collectively as "The Morrills." Rare people, or so I think, and now I wonder if we think all people rare when we are children, and later, only those we knew were rare, while new acquaintances are all alike, without distinguishing characteristics. Perhaps, and if so, what matter?

The new owner was mopping the floor behind the kidney-shaped bar. "Just give me a sec," he said, "usually I don't open till four."

"Take your time," I assured him, and he did. He mopped, emptied his trash cans beneath the bar, stocked his coolers with bottled beer. He noticed an oversight in the midst of preparing our drinks, so abandoned them while he filled several little plastic dishes with maraschino cherries, olives, and pickled onions. He distributed fistfuls of swizzle sticks at strategic junctures along the bartop.

"Where's the Morrills?" Lynne didn't like his Tom Collins.

"Oh long gone," he said. "He died, you know, better than three years ago just after Labor Day. Mrs. tried to run it another year, but I bought her out two years back. She still comes in once in a while. Stop around tonight, we have a combo. You'll just as likely see her here."

"We'll try to," I lied. Since Mr. was dead, I did not wish to see her.

He had embellished the interior. The slot machines were gone (state statute) where my mother had allowed me to lose a few dimes in an evening. The cigarette machine used to be a tall, teetering, plunger-operated thing with a mirror for customers, and it returned pennies inside the cellophane wrappers before prices climbed after the war—when cigarettes were plentiful again. His new machine glowed hazily like a computer, artificial ivy potted above it. No mirror.

There were four martini glasses upside down on the back bar with stems twisted as if they had melted, then cooled quickly. There were three dolls dressed respectively in the uniforms of the Milwaukee Braves, the New York Yankees, and an umpire, depicting a tableau disagreement at the plate. There was a picture of a man with bulbous red nose, tousled hair, and four blurred, liquid sets of eyes, and the caption, *Who's Had Enough?* And a plaster cast of Ferdinand the Bull, sitting demure on his haunches. The painting was badly done, the artist (or machine) having slipped and given Ferdinand a partial moustache. Mr. Morrill.

His first name was Wilson, called Witz. The perspective of my memory gives me a worm's-eye view of him. He stood close to the bar, so had no body below his upper diaphragm. He drank with his patrons, with style, blending the professional quaffer with the purely convivial, personally indulgent. He wore glasses with gold frames, so his eyes were distorted. His moustache was his personal symbol.

It was two spikes, waxed, standing straight away from their roots directly under his nose, black lined with gray, and if talk turned to beards or moustaches, he ran his tongue behind his upper lip and the waxed spines moved like horns. When my mother brought me along to stand next to her stool as she killed a couple of hours drinking beer and smoking, he never asked my preference, but poured me a glass of uncarbonated orange soda, a local product, delicious but not quenching. I believe he wore a gold ring with amethyst or ruby on a little finger. He addressed everyone as "folks." "What will you have, folks?" "Goodnight, folks." His lips were always wet, as though he had perennially just finished a long drink, and he spoke smoothly, with little movement in his lips—but I cannot remember anything else he ever said.

"We're having the band in again tonight," the new owner said.

"What kind of music do they play?" Lynne asked him.

"Oh, everything. Three kids from over at Berlin. We had all the gals here doing the limbo under a broomstick last night. Craziest thing you ever saw—" His eyes ignited, and he ceased speaking to dream of them.

In an alcove I saw microphones and some guitar amplifiers. There was a stack of silly hats they perhaps used to accentuate the varying moods of their music: sailor, beachboy, dunce, Napoleon.

"Does Mrs. Morrill still play?" I asked him.

"Now and again she sits down to the piano if anyone feels like singing."

I detest group sings. When compelled, I smile and move my lips, but I make no sound; a small man's protest against anonymity in masses, to be sure. But now I lie to myself, say I enjoyed them when I was small.

The ornate upright piano was still in the tavern. The wooden foliage and grapes had been painted pea green to cover a scarred finish. Mrs. Morrill played in the evenings, and once or twice I was there when her husband took a violin from its case, and mugging, placed a velvet square of cloth under his chin before accompanying his wife. I don't know that they played well. I don't remember what songs they did.

My mother sometimes bought Mrs. Morrill a drink, and she astounded me by tossing off a shot of whiskey truck-driver fashion, chasing it with a sip of plain water. She wore extreme summer dresses, puff sleeves, low necklines, tight bodices, polka-dot prints.

"My wife plays the piano," I told the man.

"Oh come on," she said.

"Feel free," he said. "Go ahead."

She looked over the sheet music stored in the piano bench, finally played some old show tunes from the 1930s. The piano was not in tune—Lynne was not in practice, and of course, it was not the same, which is why I wanted to hear it—because I knew it would not be. In absence there is presence.

"Come again," he said, opening the Venetian blinds.

"We will."

There are really two cottages. The little one, at the top of the hill, was once a barber shop in Mount Morris, a small nearby town. It was moved to the lake intact at least before 1940, when my father bought the property, just before he died. In it there is a wood stove, lights, table and chairs, and a rough double bunk bed. I have awakened there in the morning and lain in the upper bunk, looking over the sideboard at the linoleum on the floor and imagining it strewn with hair clippings. I opened it just to check the inside and found the bunk no higher than my chin now.

Barber shops are warm, florescent-lit, spicy with the odor of talc and creams and hair tonic, precise with the sound of sharp scissors and the flat stropping of razors. The little cottage was musty, close, damp, dark, and the floor creaked under my shoes. The lock was stiff with rust; I bent the key opening it.

A rough set of stairs are cut into the slope that leads down to the lower, larger cottage. The property is filled with trees—Norwegian, white, and jack pine. The needled boughs have grown out over the stairs, and we went slowly for fear the logs that edge each step were rotted and unsafe. I used to charge down that slope, leaping high to span three or four steps at a time, and my mother told me the windows in the lower cottage shook when I landed. Twenty years older, better than twice as heavy, I could never again hope to shake the earth with my footsteps. Which of us can?

Poison ivy and milkweed have overgrown the rock garden my mother built with stones taken from our lot. Her iris, pansies, and lilies of the valley have succumbed to long freezing winters. I found the stone I painted with my initials and the date. AGS 7/6/44. Faded, and I cannot remember if I put the day or the month first, June or July. I painted the rock with the edge of a small sash brush, the paint a metallic red that I'd found in the boat locker beneath the lower cottage. My hand and the brush were small, the paint thick and bright, glistening in the sun, the beach glittering with sandy reflecting crystals. The rock seemed broad, a flat side big enough to contain the statistics of my life. I turned it over with the toe of my shoe.

Lynne would do no sunbathing on our beach. The level of the spring-fed lake had gone down ten or twelve feet since I last saw it. Cattails and sawgrass had sprung up in the exposed bottom, where frogs moved. I found the black-gray ash pit where my mother and I often cooked wieners, and Lynne found a table knife that must have fallen from a paper plate as my mother and I carried them back into the cottage to burn in the stove.

Our pier had heaved, buckled, the planks splintered by the winter ice. Leaves filled the bottom near the shore, spawning season over, the scooped-out nests empty. I told Lynne of catching a legal limit of panfish, crappies, sunfish, and bluegills from the end of the pier, finding some with roe bulging their stomachs, spilling out like golden cereal when I cleaned them, and some with their tailfins worn off in the slow process of nest-making. We must both have said something about the cycle of nature, or maternal instinct, something like that.

After the airing of the cottage, a fire of pine cones to dry out the beaverboard paneling, a trip to Wautoma (two and a half miles) for groceries, eating—time to rummage. I had fled books and games, and searching, I found, of course, books and games.

I read a 1943 *Reader's Digest*, something about the power wielded by a group of U.S. senators called the "Silver Senators," men from the Southwest whose influence was out of balance with the numbers of their constituents. I began another calling on Americans to wake up to the fact that automobile bumper guards constituted an untapped source of scrap steel—I asked my wife if she thought she'd ever seen a car with a wooden bumper during the war.

Too much to read: five volumes from the *Bomba the Jungle Boy* series, bound in yellow, my name printed in each one in pencil, the date 1942, Christmas. One volume from the *Hardy Boys* mystery series. Paperback novels that had cost only a quarter. Anniversary editions of the *Saturday Evening Post*, Ben Franklin on each cover. Too much and too many: already I forget.

And games. Lynne has always disliked the literary quiz (No, I'm not William Blake). In one drawer I found Chinese checkers, Pieces of Eight, a canasta deck, pinochle deck, bridge scorepads, a sheaf of Monopoly money, a deck of Author cards. We did not stay up late. Fresh air is exhausting when it comes laden with the past.

Lynne was soon asleep. She was not involved in this. I lay awake beside her and remembered the cry of a hoot owl in a tree at the corner of the cottage because it was *not* there that night. I waited for the scurry of a rodent in the space between the ceiling and the roof because I knew it would not be there. I listened to the wind off the lake stir the pine branches, a long insistent hush that became like rain as it continued, and finally insinuated its message, saying: sleep.

The next day we hiked down the road to the Moose Tavern, but the owner was forewarned by yesterday, and his door was locked. *Open at 4 PM* his sign said. But on the way back to the cottage we met a man who knew me once. He caught me and two friends smoking in his boathouse and promptly reported it to our parents that same day—I must have been twelve. He was examining some rows of sweetcorn cultivated near the road on his lot.

"Hello, Mr. Schley," I said. I advanced, wondering if he would remember the incident, hold it against me still. I put out my hand.

"Hello," he said, and regarded me from the fastness of his corn. He touched his ear as if selecting the right name, face, and year. "I know you, don't I?" he said.

"I hope so. Smoking in your boathouse once. I used to play with the boy next door to you years ago—Ziebel. Do his folks still come up here from Indiana?"

"Spruill," he said vindictively, mistaken. "Now I know you. You caused hell all the time I remember. Spruill." He did not put out his hand.

"No," I said, "I'm Sunderlage. Allen Sunderlage. Spruill was the other one. He lived further on down—his folks lived in Minneapolis during the year, but his mother summered here."

"Is that right," he said, and probably suspected I lied. "What do you do with yourself now?"

"I'm a teacher. I will be in September. I teach English. In college." He must have thought I considered it mitigating. "This is my wife," I said.

"Never thought you'd be a teacher, Spruill," he said. We left him with his corn, declaring he had to go on to see what hornworms had done to his tomatoes.

"He certainly *must* be senile," Lynne said. "How else could he forget your name right after you told him?"

"Maybe he is a little bit. He didn't used to be. He's lived up here all year around for years. Anyway I don't blame him for remembering Spruill. He did cause hell all the time." He did. He taught me and Ziebel (Ziebel went to Korea to be killed, in 1952) to do forbidden things, and to glory in the reminiscence of having done them. He always managed to come off well when we were caught.

He persuaded us to sneak into the county fair in Wautoma one July, and when a farmer wearing a fair official's ribbon on his coveralls collared us, he performed brilliantly, crying real tears in remorse. We were released, and to prove it had been an act, he did it again for Ziebel and me.

He was the only one to follow a pattern. There was no logic in Ziebel's death in Korea (his unit was accidentally shelled by their own artillery). I recall no omen in my past explaining my vocation. But Spruill ran to form. He married, fathered a daughter when he was nineteen, divorced when he was twenty, and remarried again in Las Vegas, where the last I knew he dealt cards—married to a showgirl.

"Maybe you're an easy face to forget," Lynne said.

"I blend."

That night ended it. The motels, drive-in custard stands (also a drive-in movie), and gas stations that had proliferated along the highways in the area had already begun to remind me of footnotes and textual references. An even sameness in the dry hot weather began to pervade and influence my thoughts. The late afternoon and evening that we spent at the big resort on the other end of the lake finished it. We stayed less than two days.

Tourism is big business now in Waushara County (I don't know that the name is Indian, but it is also the name of the local bottling company that used to make uncarbonated orange soda). The resort beach is enclosed now by a cyclone fence and it cost Lynne a quarter to lie in the sun on a blanket.

I think it was the crowds that did it. Years ago, late afternoon meant a warm mood of sleep to the adults on the lake. Now there is no time. I used to hike to the resort with my friends, Ziebel and Spruill, and find no more than half a dozen cars parked along the road that runs through the resort grounds from the highway. Half of them belonged to high school boys from Wautoma who failed to find summer jobs. The resort bar was nearly empty until nightfall, and the owner then, a man named Plager, thin and bald, went for a daily swim in the lake.

In those days (before insurance rates mushroomed) he kept a huge forty-foot slide anchored in ten feet of water at his beach. There was a story that he won a bet by going down the slide naked at high noon, so I was anxious not to miss it if it happened again; it never did. The slide is gone (insurance rates), and so is Plager. The beach was horribly overcrowded.

The water moved with bawling, splashing children, fat mothers who bobbed up and down with terrified babies in their arms, a growth of bathing caps. Lynne had to pick her way among the peeling sunbathers on the sand who had come early and staked claims with blankets, hampers, bottles of suntan creams and lotions, soda and beer. She waved to me from the inferior patch of sand and grass she found near a corner in the fence, donning her sunglasses, anonymous immediately.

I went to the pavilion. Its sides were open twenty years ago. Birds nested in the exposed rafters and roof beams, and at night mosquitoes ignored the roof's border of yellow light bulbs, invading to sting the dancers. Now there are thin walls to keep anyone from seeing the dancers, and electrified wire grates that zap insects to ashes upon contact.

Afternoons my friends and I sat near the jukebox and drank soda, small change burning holes in our pockets. In a moment of madness I have broken the solid presence of a fifty-cent piece into smooth, ephemeral nickels, and fed them vainly to the jukebox, while pairs of girls I neither knew nor admired experimented with new jitterbug steps.

An afternoon passed, long and slow, so large around the three of us there was no possibility of breaking away from it. There was time, and we were at the center of it, and like ourselves, it would surely never end.

Saturdays Mr. Plager brought three-piece combos from as far away as Plainfield or even Oshkosh, and a dance was held. Teenagers paid the admission, received a stamp on the backs of their hands that glowed purple under a special lamp. The girls, tanned golden legs bursting fully out of their short shorts, in sweatshirts from fraternities at Big Ten universities, danced with each other over the floor Plager had salted with resin powder sprinkled from a can, their feet scuffing invitingly. My friends and I stood up to the levels of the boys' biceps, bared, tee-shirt sleeves rolled up and over their shoulders. They smoked and frowned at the dancing girls, and occasionally turned away to comb their hair.

When the war was on, young men were scarce, and when a soldier or sailor on leave showed up, he was sure to wear his uniform, to dance with the girls, to ignore the boys too young for the draft who sneered at uniforms.

Now there is no time. Whole families crowd around the pavilion, sunglasses bubbling their eyes, yachting caps, sticky popsicles dropping from small hands, hurried, worried looks on their faces. They stand in lines to eat things and spend their money. The chant of the resort's cash registers is constant. And even I have no time to look closely at their faces and see what they really look like. I know I'm in a hurry, pressed; I have to get back to Chicago. I was so long waiting for service in the packed bar that I only had my third drink when Lynne joined me from the beach, a touch of red on the bridge of her nose.

"It's a madhouse," she said.

"Give them a break," I told her. "They work hard, they want to play hard."

"This isn't a tavern, it's a vending machine."

"This is the machine age." Around us, people blinked smoke out of their eyes, laughed loudly, and made small piles of their coins and cigarette cases in front of them on the bartop. The new owner, a burly Pole who grew over-solvent in a south side Milwaukee tavern, poured whiskey without spilling, the volume measured by a jigger-cap. Hoses ran from pressurized tanks, and a four-tubed spigot squirted four different mixes at the touch of the proper button.

"How's business?" I asked him.

"Another one?" he said, poised over my empty glass.

"Forget it."

A beer bar has been added for teenagers. They get frisky as the hour grows late, and a rock-and-roll band twanging incessantly heats their thin blood. When their conversations lag, the patrons around us look out the window to watch a fistfight or two, and the owner sighs, dries his hands, and goes outside to knock their belligerent heads together, restoring order.

"You've got a problem with those kids," my wife said to him.

"My bouncer's gone to a wedding," he complains.

"Do you want to stop at the Moose place on our way back?" Lynne asked me.

"No, indeed not. Let's head for home. Chicago, not the cottage."

"Tonight? Right now?"

"Yep. I've seen enough."

"Give me a clue as to what you're thinking about sometime, will you?" she said.

So we closed up the cottage that night and drove back to my mother's in Chicago. The drive silent, our Hudson a strange roaring thing in the darkness, through all the towns with wonderful names.

"You didn't stay long," my mother said, glad to see us back.

"I can always go back," I said. And I can. If, for example, I wake up one morning to find I turned forty overnight, or thirty-five, or fifty, things multiplying around me, making me small and anonymous in the contrast, I have a remedy. Halve a quantity again and again, infinitely, and still you have a half as your product.

I can go back again. And again.

Wave the Old Wave

Wally McFadden is more than just presentable when ready to go
forth and wrestle with the city for bread. Ready-made suits seem cut
specifically to solidify the beginning slackness that has set in around
his middle. He's almost unaware of this softening at age thirty-six.
His slightly large hands are smooth, and his complexion suggests
that he *could* have been in Florida recently. His hair, when he has
flattened out the spikes of sleep with Vitalis, shines a rich brown,
and the tendency toward a natural wave requires only a little mirror
coaxing.

A Parker 51 fountain pen in his jacket pocket looks like more than
a convenience on him. He inspires confidence in strangers, over-
powers them a little. If he came to sell them insurance instead of
autos (Ford Thunderbirds), they would be eager to see him whip the
pen out and compose a comprehensive life plan for them in an ex-
pensive-looking handwriting.

"Bye," Wally says to his oldest daughter, Clara, as she trails out
behind the other three. He says it as something of a challenge, to
dare the girl to answer him. He's probing the limits of his influence.
In addition, he stretches out his arms, suggests a kiss with his lips—
also something of a test.

"Bye, father," Clara says, and meets him halfway with a bacon-
tasting kiss. But no embrace. She goes, and Wally wonders: how
long is it now since his daughters—poor girls, he thinks—have called
him Daddy or Dad? No doubt it dates from the time his wife, Alice,

began calling him by his surname. Funny, he thinks ironically, how he once thought drinking was fun.

"It's ten to eight, McFadden," Alice tells him. She is at once a flurry of gathering, checking, binding her lunch bag with a rubber band. Alice teaches the fourth grade at a school different from the one the girls attend. "Do you want me to drop you off?" she asks. Oh! Wally thinks, what big suspicions you have, Grandma!

"No thanks," he says, challenging again.

"Well, I've got to run," Alice says. She'll be late, even if the car does start right away. After today, Wally will have his demonstrator again. The beauty of that is she can't take the demonstrator and make him drive their own '49 Ford. You can't sell Thunderbirds by riding around in anything but.

"What am I smoking today, O.P.B.'s?" Wally says. Alice stops at the kitchen door, unsnaps her purse. Give thanks to wherefrom all good things come, Wally says to himself. Just like payday in the army. Alice does so well with the finances, Wally sometimes wonders if she doesn't have her own printing press somewhere. Think of that!

He nearly laughs. Alice sneaking from her classroom, down to some dirty corner of the boiler room for an ostensible smoke, there cranking out thirty or forty bucks to efficiently cover a shortage someplace in the system.

"Here," Alice says; then, "No, wait. Here." She starts to give him a dollar, perhaps feels her conscience, gives him two. But by God! he thinks, if she didn't look to see how many cigarettes she had first! Seeing if she couldn't get off with giving him the article instead of the money.

You're a sly dog, Alice old girl, he thinks. But not sly enough. He remembers telling Vic Hoar, the sales manager at Morgan Ford, the day he was fired—he had been drunk of course. Hoar had said: "When the hell you going to make up your mind you're going to have to work for a living like the rest of us, Wally?" Wally had smiled at him, pretending to examine the fifteen-cent cigar he was smoking, replied: *Hoar, my friend* (to himself, Wally always spelled it w-h-o-r-e), *I ask you, why should I work for twenty bucks a day when I can steal ten a day from my wife?*

"Say hello to Vic for me," Alice says, bundles gathered. Did she imply, Wally wonders, that I should tell him thanks too? And now goodbye. Wally can do it blind if need be. He really does do it blind, relying on the fact that movie stars always close their eyes before they kiss in a picture.

He closes his eyes, puckers his lips, much in the way he puckers after tossing off a shot of bottom-shelf whiskey (Charter Oak, Cream of Kentucky). He can do that pucker in his sleep. Like a robot. He bends slightly forward, stiffly efficient as a mechanical man, and smacks off a kiss for Alice. Their puckers meet, bounce.

This is when Wally feels the weakest. He is trapped by the cross-lines of his context. He became most aware of it during the long lay-off from work that ends this morning, this so real, so gloomy Monday morning. It is that Alice puckers, and he, not wanting to, but knowing still that he will, follows through on command. I am a wage slave, he thinks. And what the hell kind of payment is this?

He kisses Alice's buck-tooth puckers, and he cannot do it without wondering why he does not feel the edges of her teeth against his lips. Each time, as now, when he kisses Alice away to work, he has a vision of his context, the human side of it. Context of Wally McFadden, human-wise.

The vision of his wife and four daughters, standing in a row, arranged by order of age and height, oldest and tallest on the left. Like a set of plaster dolls, won at a grotesque carnival. Five thin, long types. They all seem too narrow for natural childbirth. Five with fuzzy, frizzy hair that won't stay in place, with wrinkles in their clothes where the cloth won't hang smooth over such bony joints. How do you tell them apart?

Easy. Alice is the one without crossed eyes. They have never yet seen fit to afford the operation for the girls. No doubt their crossed eyes bring them much misery at school.

Wally begins to feel just a bit angry with Alice gone now. At himself. He begins to formulate the first rocky definitions of his determination to make a go of this thing of coming back. This will be the third try at it. Can you catch the brass ring this time around, Wally old boy? he asks himself. Come on folks, let's all pull for Wally McFadden to make it this trip. Let's all root for McFadden to sell a whole fleet of new Thunderbirds so he can get those eyes uncrossed!

It comes from Wally's side. His left eye tends to wander when he's tired or drunk. Let's cheer!

Wally is amused at the idea of a telethon. Going to the bedroom, he takes the three singles, hidden from the last grocery shopping he did for Alice, and adds them to the two Alice gave him. Wally thinks: with a finski-fiver in his pocket, a man can take a little heart. He gathers up the tools of his trade, stuffing them into a leather bag, and departs, on time, to shoulder his portion, his slice of the collective responsibility of the system. He is not nearly so angry with Alice for having called Vic Hoar (whore) and arranged another chance for him. He is almost grateful.

Wiping Alice's kiss off his mouth, he thinks of a little drink to start the day with, bleeds just a bit for his cross-eyed daughters, revolts . . . then sighs, figuratively throws up his hands, plods to a bus stop.

But by the time he arrives at his place of work, Morgan Ford Sales, Inc., he has rebuilt at least a kind of nervous determination to labor hard and well, to succeed, to ultimately uncross the eyes of his daughters. He has even begun to believe there is something in the future for him too.

Vic Hoar greets him at the door of the showroom, helps him by taking the leather bag Wally carries, pumps his hand in the over-friendly fashion of the salesman, speaks warmly. "Wally baby welcome back you're looking good kid!" The sound of his given name is soothing in itself. Like all *good* salesmen, Wally really believes it means something at the moment.

Another salesman, already on the floor, looking most potentially busy in his idleness, calls out, "Hey, Highpockets! Call a cop to handle the traffic, McFadden has returned!" Wally gives him the sort of wave of the hand he gives to a customer who drives off in a new Thunderbird, a combination of *Fare thee well, friend* and *So long, sucker!* Gratitude and contempt.

"Where am I parked, Vic?" Wally asks, cracking his knuckles in eagerness to get with it. Like most worldly horses, afraid of the glue factory tomorrow, Wally welcomes the straps and buckles of the harness.

"Same old place, Number One for you, Wally," Hoar says. "How's Alice?"

"Oh great!" Visions of a set of five thin women assail him; he stiffens his back. Vic Hoar leads him to his old office, a cubicle created by the erection of three walls at one side of the showroom. The first one on the left as you enter.

Vic Hoar tells him, "Take your time and get settled—I want to see about getting you set up on the payroll . . . your mail box ready . . . take your time."

"I'll do that, Vic," Wally says, and sends the sales manager on his way with the wave. He opens his briefcase and pulls out the tools of his trade.

A desk name-plate reading WALLY MCFADDEN. Nothing more. He's had that for ages. A two-ballpoint-pen desk set, given to him one Christmas by his four daughters combined. Poor girls, he thinks again, anxious to get to business. Three or four outdated brochures on the Thunderbird line. He'll need to get new ones from Hoar (whore). A note pad which has *Things To Do* printed on the top of each sheet. He makes a note asking Hoar (whore) for the new brochure: he pens *get crap from whore*, then chuckles. A plastic sign to hang in one of the windows of his office. It reads *Out To Lunch*, and has a line drawing of a ravenous man's face, mouth full of even, horse-sized teeth, about to bite into a disembodied woman's breast. Stationery and envelopes. A small box which contains a rubber stamp and ink pad. He opens it in an attitude of confidence, makes a trial impression on his note pad.

In dark purple: *Wally McFadden, Thunderbird Specialist: The World's Greatest Automobile Salesman.*

Vic Hoar returns with an income tax and social security form for Wally to sign.

"Fill this out right away, Wally—don't want to see you end up in the poorhouse. Ha ha."

"That's right—got to look out for the family—I can always send Alice out on the street, huh? Ha ha." Wally asks him, "How's draw?"

"Samo—samo, Wally, fifty a week plus comish. Draw it every two weeks, samo-samo."

"How's the action been?"

"With the T-birds, Wally, you know, it's what you make it. I guess you know how to hustle . . . samo-samo." Hustle, Wally hears. His blood runs a little quicker, his eyes shine, he wants to snap his fingers . . . the feel is coming back.

"Watch me hustle, Vic!" Wally says, and he goes along with Hoar to pick up the new brochures, postcards, stamps, from the sales manager's secretary. Watch me hustle! His daughters are a cinch to have their eyes straightened—Alice can quit working—anything can happen when he feels like hustling.

But the action on the showroom floor is slow, nothing to inspire him. There's nothing tangible to fight, nothing of substance to get his teeth into. The vision of his cross-eyed daughters fades, blurs, loses the sharpness of reality. He writes a few postcards to addresses on the right side of town.

The cards are done in full color. A pink T-bird convertible, a young man and woman sitting in it in the driveway of a large manor house. They're waving to an equally young and attractive couple in the doorway of the manor house. Wally smiles: the female models have expressions suggesting that they have just been playfully goosed by their respective escorts. They've done it and are glad.

Wally writes half a dozen of the cards. He writes, with the Parker 51, in his expensive hand: *Hi! Interested in some exciting news about an exciting new car? Want to know how this car can be a part of your future? Want to put yourself into the picture NOW?* (paragraph) *Then see me, Wally McFadden, Morgan Ford Sales Inc.* He adds his telephone extension. Then, not quite satisfied, wanting to crown the effort, he uses his rubber stamp across the face of the cards, obliterating the shocked grins of the female models.

But the action is still slow. He cannot bring himself to do any telephoning. He thinks of wandering out on the floor. Maybe he can absorb a little brilliance from the sheen of the new autos on display. Maybe a view of himself through the showroom window will bring a prospect in from the street. Nothing much on the street either. Nothing doing. The world has come to a dead halt. All except for the needs and desires inside Wally McFadden—and, of course, his wife and four cross-eyed daughters.

He thinks he might go out on the floor, hone away the edge of his boredom on his fellow salesmen. Two of them lean against the fender of a new Falcon, peer out the window at the quiet street, so intently and silently, as if trying to pierce the stones of the building across the street, make manna flow from them. But Wally sees the dead end in that before he gets up. Nothing seems to want to help. He wonders if he's expected to move the universe with just his own shoulder.

Desperate, he goes to the secretary to get more stamps. He sits down in his cubicle and writes two cards before this isn't enough either. He's got to tell somebody. He writes: *Hi! Interested in some exciting B.S.? Want to find out the truth about what's going on between those people in the picture? Want to quit guessing and find out who really did what to who?* (paragraph) *Then see me*—Wally hesitates, thinks vaguely of the postal laws, then goes on. *I'm hiding out someplace in this city, just waiting to slip you the news* (he thought of writing *shaft*, but the postal laws)— *Look over your shoulder, I'm right behind you!*

Wally laughs aloud. The two salesmen on the floor look at him, smile, shake their heads, glance furtively in the direction of Vic Hoar's office, then begin, Wally's sure, to talk badly of him. Wally, feeling like an entertainer who's having a bad night but doesn't give a damn, shrugs, writes another card.

Excuse me for intruding on the privacy of your life with this card. But the fact of the matter is that I'm bored stiff, and yet I'm supposed to be doing something here today. Forgive me, I'm a man with a wife and four lovely daughters, trying like hell to meet my responsibilities. (paragraph) *Please ignore this card. Forget the whole thing. Burn this.* He pauses for inspiration, signs it *The Phantom.*

Unable to laugh, Wally rises and walks out onto the floor. His co-workers look expectant. No, he thinks, it's not the place. It's the same comfortable structure of brick, cement, tile, glass. The same (almost the same) waxed cars on the floor. The same active hum from the bookkeeping office in the rear. Typewriters, telephones, the intercom. *Vic Hoar . . . line six please. Mr. Hoar, line six.*

He balances, weighs critically. Vic Hoar (whore). Wife and four ugly daughters. Ugly wife and four daughters. Fifty per drawn every two weeks. Plus comish. No action. The need. The responsibility. It can't be them, he thinks. It must be me! In me! I'm weak, he decides.

Wally figures: a man can't just come back to the mill that fast, break off a bender that fast, jump right into the struggle without feeling something. My God! They expect me to hustle today. Yesterday I could barely crawl. First things first. Let me hobble a little while, huh?

He reconnoiters. Vic Hoar (whore) must be back in the shop. The switchboard girl is busy. A couple of the salesmen will see him, but so what! Wally twitches his shoulders to adjust the way his jacket sets on him, pinches his windsor knot, pivots on the tile floor, heads for the door.

"Where you off to, McFadden?"

"Got a hot lead, Wally?"

"Coffee break," Wally croaks, and closes the door behind him. He fingers the five dry bills in his pocket. He thinks: if you want a pump to give water, you have to prime it first.

He rededicates himself. Leaning against the bar of the Step-In Tap, four doors down from Morgan Ford Sales Inc., he feels fresh life tingle through his extremities. The cheap whiskey pucker, the kiss-Alice pucker, is still on his lips. Joints fluid, tongue quick and oily in his mouth, fumes of the drink rising from his palate, he begins to love the life around him. He would like to sell something to everyone!

Sally, the bartender, answers the telephone. "I'll see," she says. Wally thinks her orange-bleached hair almost lovely in the uncertain light. "McFadden," she asks him, smothering the receiver in her pillow bosoms, "are you in?"

"To whom?"

"Vic Hoar. Pee-oh'd sounding."

"Let's hear him," Wally says. The receiver is still warm from Sally as he puts it to his ear. "What'ya got, Vic? Is that right? I guess so, yes. In a min, Vic."

"Is he hot?" Sally asks him. "Catch one on me before you go."

"Don't hold me back, Sal," he says, waving back the offered shot, "don't hold me back, lover. Vic says he's got a live one . . . he needs a closer, baby, so watch me hustle!"

The action has picked up by the time he returns. His cheeks are rosied by the wind and the drinks. He enters like a rush of that brisk, refreshing autumn air. His hand is extended when he is yet two paces from Vic Hoar and the prospect. He is hustling.

Wally's grip is the grip that gratifies. His hand is dry, skin the browned texture of wealthy people, one and one-half pumps of the arm. He uses the possessive mode, both hands, his left gripping Mr. Hearkins, the prospect, by the wrist, tenderly but positively.

"Glad for your acquaintance," Wally says, meaning it.

"I'm only just kind of getting the lay of the land you might say," Mr. Hearkins says. A nothing, a no place, Wally thinks, taking in the fat man with little pig eyes set deep above his red cheeks—blue boozer's veins in his face at close range—the sunglasses case on his belt—a fringed buckskin jacket, modified cowboy boots. You'll be easy! Wally thinks. He chalks Mr. Hearkins up, imaginatively carts his head home to show to Alice as proof of how he hustles.

"Give him the third degree, Mr. Hearkins," Vic Hoar says; "he's supposed to have all the answers."

"I always like to dicker . . . ha ha," Mr. Hearkins says. "My first name's Elsmer—most people don't catch it right off."

Wally puts Elsmer Hearkins through his paces. Surprises him by handing the keys to a demonstrator over to him, holding the front door open for him to drive—without asking. It flatters. Wally knows. "She insured? Ha ha," Hearkins says.

The pitch. The long run of statistics. What he doesn't know or remember, Wally makes up. Talking as they drive, Wally watches him closely, and he sees beneath the fringed buckskin jacket and sunglasses and cowboy boots. He finds his softness, fingers it.

He sees the gold band Hearkins wears, the slightly worried, cracking lines in his face, the false set of his fat jaw as he drives the expensive car as if it was made of china. Wally knows he has caught Mr. Elsmer Hearkins, citified hick, putting himself up on the block for measurement—measuring himself, his poor fat self, against the value of an overpriced auto. So he plays on his fear of being found short in the analysis. As he talks, Wally calculates the commission needed to correct four pairs of crossed eyes and five bruised hearts, to mellow five vengeant souls—the number of Elsmers it will take to do it.

"Seriously now, Elsmer," he says, "why should we kid? You're not just shopping for a car—*anybody* does that. I know it and you know it. We both know you're not just looking for transportation when you come to see the kind of wheels I handle, right?"

"Oh yes," Hearkins says, daring to take his pig eyes from his driving for a split second to smile.

"And it's not the money—if you're worried about gas mileage you don't come looking at this car, right?"

"Well, that's a big bite—you have to see your way clear on the money, Wally (Wally has him on first names)," Hearkins says, squirming his bottom on the comfortable seat, caressing the wheel, inhaling the smell of the upholstery. Wally sees the fear. His instincts tell him two ways: Oh, how easy for you, Wally boy, Wallace my boy, how easy! And: Take him back. Let him go. Send him home.

"Essentially," Wally says, twisting the knife, "it's a matter of matching yourself up with the kind of context you live in, right?"

"I'd say so, maybe," Hearkins says with doubt.

"Kay," Wally says. And yet, he can't quite bring himself to snap it off, get Elsmer Hearkins' signature on a deal. He looks at Elsmer Hearkins, strips him of his defenses, his cowboy boots and too-big, too-aviator-style shades, fringed buckskin jacket. He pities his nakedness in the city. He pinches his windsor knot again, to be sure he himself is dressed. He needs time—he gives Elsmer Hearkins a break, a reprieve, and they stop in at the Step-In.

In a short time he has Hearkins trembling between the fear of buying and the fear of not daring to. It is interesting to Wally just to see his mark quiver. "A man," Wally says, testing, over the second drink, "has to come to grips with a decision, right? Now I can tell you, in this business, if I know anything, it's people. You admit that? Thing is, a man like yourself, you've got to come down to a decision—you have all the facts—a man knows whether he's ready to make the splash or not—" Sally listens to him in admiration. "—you and I don't have to crap each other, Elsmer, because you might as well know I can look right into your heart and tell what's going to be—I know people, I tell you." Hearkins lowers his eyes, fiddles with his drink, drinks it too fast.

Wally is aghast. He *can* look right into him. And more, make him jump either way he wants him to. It's only a matter of deciding.

"I have to see my way clear on the money—be sure," Mr. Hearkins says. Sally is smirking with admiration. Wally fights a desire to take him out of sheer pride.

After all, he thinks, there's always tomorrow—someone can come in on the floor whose fat little heart won't burst over having a T-bird. Someone might just come in who buys automobiles like Alice buys shoes for the girls.

"See, Elsmer," Wally says, "a salesman *pushes* used cars, your ordinary cars, get me? That's the jungle, dog eat dog—but my product, all I have to do is show it to advantage—it does the rest." After four drinks, Wally sighs to see Mr. Hearkins buy a round. If you can make them buy for you, you can make them do anything, he knows. He thinks of making Hearkins happy, decides he'd like to. And he means it.

The new brochures spread out in front of him, the slick color photos of the autos he can't match up to screaming at him in a host of living prints, Elsmer Hearkins whimpers before admiring Sally, says, "See, Wally, I've got to consider my obligations. . . ."

Wally McFadden considers his obligations. He is obligated, every inch of him, to everyone from the U.S. government all the way down to his daughters. He's obligated, all the way, right up to the hilt of his expected mortality, projected on into infinity. Every last buck, every dollar of draw, every cent percent of commission on sales, every bonus in every sales contest—from the sweat off my back to the pennies on my dead eyes, I owe. God help me, Wally thinks, his blood moving. *I'm* the only anybody I don't owe something to!

"Real dollars and cents, Wally," Elsmer Hearkins says, not knowing he's been set free to thrash about a while longer, until the next hungry tiger licks his chops over his soft fatness, "the bigger the price, the bigger the profit, isn't that so?"

Where's my profit? Wally asks himself. No money. It's not the halves, quarters, singles I sneak out of the grocery money—Jesus! I won't settle for that! My children? Diminishing returns, he decides; they're getting older every day. Poor things, he thinks, sad that he doesn't love them enough to sacrifice Hearkins to them. A fat goat too. He glances in the back-bar mirror, sees how his left eye has begun to wander off center. Alice is only my manager.

"A man's got to be careful," Hearkins says now, growing more verbal, thinking, sensing he might escape.

Dear Mr. Elsmer Hearkins, Wally sees himself writing, *Take my advice and hurry home . . . to your careful home, and let them say it doesn't matter what you drive—and please don't talk to strangers if you don't want to get eaten up before you get there.*

"You must admit that, Wally," Elsmer says.

Dear Wally McFadden, he writes, *Don't you think you ought to look about through the empty whiskey bottles to see what's been left to you by the good fairy? Hadn't you better ask when payday is in this outfit?*

Hearkins has beat a retreat to the men's room. "Telephone, Wally," Sally says to him.

"Who?" He is dubious about being in to anyone at all.

"Your spouse—I think. Are you in?"

Wally McFadden closes his eyes, tries to find his way back to the house, to this morning when he vowed he'd be good. Let's see: the lawn needs cutting, but not if we get an early snow. The storm windows don't need to go up; they're still up from last winter. Shrewd, Wally boy!

"Well?"

"Really, you can't blame a fellow, Wally," Hearkins says on his timid return from the toilet. Can you make it back? Wally asks himself. Can you forget what you know, take this Elsmer Whatzis in your teeth, bleed him? There's Alice and the girls. Check. And Vic Hoar (whore). Check. Wally laughs, a wheezing, snide, self-searched, foregone-conclusion laugh. How soon would it be that a letter would reach her if I wrote right tonight? It is dusk outside now, overcast. The waxed shine of the T-bird demonstrator is dull, seen through the window of the Step-In.

"I'll tell her you left for work," Sally says.

Wally quickly takes the receiver, one last effort to see if he can't remember—and if he can't forget.

"Say, it's late!" Hearkins says, not knowing he's safe.

"Frzz-frzz," Wally says into the phone, imitating the sound of Alice beating her stiff hair into submission in front of her vanity mirror in the cold of Monday mornings—as if she enjoyed them. He has a waiting, quizzical look on his handsome face.

"Is that you, McFadden?" he hears a thin, angular voice say. He hands the receiver to Sally, and she sets it in the cradle, blocking the way back. A debt you'll never pay, Wallace Mitchell McFadden, he thinks. But she owed me a name at least. Or I owe it to myself. A test of sorts. . . .

"Elsmer," he says to the pardoned mark, "Elsmer," pronouncing his given name generously, "Elsmer," as he prods him out the door, "Elsmer, go home and wait for me and only me to call you about the car—no, don't talk to any salesmen—of anything—until you hear from me. How? You bet, Elsmer, you bet!" and he waves him off down the street with a mixture of feeling: half love, half pity. Poor soul, Elsmer, he thinks after him.

"Catch one on me, Wally," Sally says to him. "My God, Wally, you could charm the birds out of the trees I think!" And he refuses her, waves her away on his way out.

The sales manager awaits him. "Did you get the demo in without piling it up?"

"Way ahead of you, Vic—you have to hustle—see, I *knew* I was too looped to drive—it's sitting in front of Sally's."

"And?"

"Save it. I already quit, about ten minutes ago."

"Oh, this is sweet, McFadden," Vic says as he stands in the doorway of his glass cubicle, watches Wally ram his belongings, his tools, into his briefcase. He's more ashamed, Wally thinks, than he is angry.

"Mail my check to Alice."

"You got no check."

"Then we're even, huh?"

"Going back to creeping dimes from Alice?"

"I'm too old to swipe dimes. I swipe dollars when I put my mind to it . . . but you have to be fast. I'm too slow. You have to hustle. It's a hard world, Vic." He smiles at Hoar (whore). "Loan me a fin, Vic."

"For what?"

"For anything. Who cares. For booze. For me." Wally laughs, the wheezing laugh—is shocked when Vic gives him the money.

"What in the hell are you going to do, you crud?" Vic asks him as Wally pauses in the doorway, the cold air coming into the showroom, through the gaps he doesn't fill. Wally stares. If he concentrates, he can make that wild eye sit right in place. The hell with it. It roams free. But he is touched at Hoar's (whore's) concern. It's odd, he thinks, you find these little dividends when you least expect them.

"Think I'll go into business for myself—wanna buy some stock?"

"No thanks."

"No faith, huh?" He steps out into the windy street. Under his arm he clutches his bag of tools, his tricks. He looks to the left, looks to the right, hesitates, shrugs, goes right, away from the location of Sally's Step-In. Not knowing where he's going, except sure he'll end up someplace—he imagines everyone does—he turns back once, looks at Vic in the doorway, surrounded by the bright showroom lights, the glass and steel and brick. Wally feels his strongest.

And he waves. Once. The old wave.

Gold Moments and Victory Beer

The way it happened, Big Edwards just leaned forward in his chair, reached out, and slapped Smitty smack across his tan face. "There," he said, like he'd taken a dare on something. "There" was all he said. I was facing the both of them, chair sideways to the damp table filled with pitchers of victory beer, so I saw it all. I was always seeing everything. Which is one of my troubles.

Ray Botts didn't see it. He was harping about the mess somebody made washing up after the game in the men's toilet. He nodded his round head in the direction of the toilet and said, sullen, "Who was it crudded up the sink for the Christ's sakes?"

Fred Jantke saw. He looked at Edwards, but he wasn't for doing anything about it just yet. "What the hell was that for?" was all he had to say. Ray Botts still didn't notice anything. He looked at me, accusing.

"Tee-bow," he said, "is that you, dirtied up the sink?" I didn't answer, waiting for Smitty to pick it up or leave it.

The way it happened, Big Edwards had said to him: "You know, Smith, I get on the force now, I'm in a position for hanging you if I feel like it."

Smitty didn't smile, not even the cynical ten-dollar smile. He kept his eyes on Edwards, knowing I was watching him, and said, "You're a liar and a eee-lapper, a four-day creeper and a turd-snapper." The Big Edwards peered at him like he didn't see him any better than he heard him. He leaned forward, peered, then slapped him smack in the face.

Well, I thought to myself, what's the difference anyway? I always see everything; I'm always watching. What's the use of anything anyway? I thought. That's about when I was feeling the lowest about everything, right after he slapped Smitty.

Even coming back from Pumping Station Field in Fred Jantke's car, naturally having won, I was pretty sour. Not that there wasn't some good feeling too. Nothing can ever sour everything for me.

We won of course—Edwards is without fail the best fastpitch softball pitcher in the County Fastpitch League, and likely one of the three, four best in the state. And I had a few good moments. Three for four, one double that faster I could've stretched to third—no apology, since my arm from right field and my stick make up for lacking speed. Speed is my short suit; I admit it.

There's undeniable good moments: seeing it from out in right field, the sun bouncing off Edwards' sweated red forehead, that big man shrugging his shoulders to let out his breath as he toes the rubber, and then that big arm comes around, the little flap sound it makes when his hand brushes his pant leg to meet underhand regulations, the sharp *pop* sound when the ball lands in Fred Jantke's glove behind the plate—hearing it almost before I see the batter twist his back trying for the pitch. I hear the infield talk when they whip it around the horn after Edwards fans another batter, a little applause from the stands behind the screen, and then Ray Botts comes off the bench with his clipboard in his hand to wave us outfielders around to position for the next man up if Edwards hasn't already fanned the entire side.

When I'm sticking too. I like grinding my spikes in deep in the box, and I keep taking practice cuts right up until the pitcher starts his motion. I fox the hell out of them, because I can choke up on the bat to place the ball while it's already coming at me. That kind of fast I have. I can feel it when it's right, the second I hit that six-inch inseam ball. And no denying I like to hear the clapping and the shouts from the stands, and what they say from the bench. On first base, Ray Botts in the coaching box pats me on the fanny and starts putting it to the pitcher to watch me like as if I was likely to steal.

Good, running in to help pick up mitts and bats in the long canvas bag with *Axel's Inn* on the side in white paint that's faded to look almost like chalk after nearly three seasons. Loading up in the cars to get to Axel's, winning team serves the beer, loser's sponsor pays. Undeniable.

In the car heading for the tavern, Fred Jantke spat out the window expertly and said to Ray Botts, our manager-coach-statistician-utility player, "RayBotts, for Christ's sakes, why you don't put in a official protest, them em-pires! they don't see nothing." He grabbed the necker's knob on the wheel and steered around a safety island.

"Quit bitching," Ray Botts said. "Edwards goes into police school now, he'll be pitching for the police department, you'll have something to holler about. Then it's honeymoon all over for us, you'll have something to cry for."

Really? I ask myself. Then I'm sour. That's how I get that way. Fred Jantke cleared his throat to hawk again. Ray Botts was busy in the official scorekeeper's book. It felt like no breeze came in the open car windows. I'm sour as hell.

Big Edwards wants to be a cop, goes to police school, so what? So Axel's Inn doesn't win every Saturday afternoon anymore. So we don't grab off the county trophy every year. We don't grab off a trophy in the regionals, likely the sectionals too, this year. That's so what. And more: where now how there's this fair-to-good chance on the state invitational championship (individual engraved plaques as big as meat platters), without Big Edwards there is positively no chance. Which is also so what.

Without Edwards we're just another tavern team, a few trophies over the bar, tarnishing a little each year. Without Edwards we're just what we are, I'm thinking. That's so what. Christ, I am sour.

"As a team we hit .379 so far the season," Ray Botts said.

"It ain't hitting counts, RayBotts," Fred Jantke said.

"Tee-bow," Ray Botts said, "you're sticking a wicked .505. That's good for maybe third, fourth in the league." I opened the back window all the way and spat, hoping I didn't streak the rear fender. He was trying to say something cheerful.

"You lose Edwards," I had to say, "you won't care what nobody's sticking."

Some more of my moments: coming into Axel's. I walk behind

Edwards, who rides with Voss because Voss has a convertible. I walk in behind him, seeing those shoulders fill the doorway, standing only high enough on him to look at the back of his red neck, and I think how here is the best softball pitcher of maybe an entire state, and I am possibly the third leading percentage hitter in the county league, and I have to hold myself back, slow down so as not to crowd into the back of Edwards' sweaty jersey, white felt letters on green, Axel's Inn, because I feel like I'm glowing and would burn anyone who touches me.

Inside I wave first to Les, the regular bartender, who is in the middle of saying to Edwards, "You put them away, Big Ed?" All unnecessary. I spot Schneider, the beat cop, sitting at the bar, deadheading on duty of course. I clown a bit to work out of what I feel because I can hardly stand it. I yank Schneider's cop's hat off the back of his head and plunk it down on Edwards from behind. "Schneider," I say, "look what's coming on the police force these days."

"For the Christ's sakes," Schneider says, who could care less.

Edwards obliges. He turns the hat sideways, steps to the end of the bar, pounds his fist and snarls at Les, "Everybody outta da pool!"

"Hey Les," says Voss, a middling good first sacker, "this means he gets free drinks and scoff like Schneider, right?"

"Where's my graft?" Edwards snarls.

"That'll be the day I get graft," Schneider slurs.

Edwards sailed the hat back down the bar to him. Ray Botts went behind the bar to see to tapping the victory barrel. "You all set now, Big Ed?" Les asked.

"Week and a half I report to orientation. They got the academy right downtown in the Safety Building annex. Eight hours a day, five days a week, then you go on duty, but on probation," Edwards said. He reached his long arm behind the bar to take a fistful of hard-boiled eggs from the wire rack.

"Have fun is all I say," Schneider said, having been lucky enough to become a cop when the standards were lower.

I look up above the bar at the row of gold trophies on the shelf, dusted regularly by Les. All sizes, and the biggest the County Fast-pitch League traveler, which remains here permanent, with names engraved, when we win it for the third season in a row this year.

Whatever way they list us, alphabetical, batting order, I'll be there: *Thibault, George.* In gold.

I'm looking at the row of gold above the back-bar mirror, seeing my name, gold on gold, and I'm glowing again. Edwards is talking to Les and Schneider, Voss is calling for the Sheepshead cards, Ray Botts swearing at a clumsy beertapper . . . with this year's championship already cinched, forever and forever, my name's in gold at Axel's Inn, and all the regulars and chance stoppers-in will see my name if they look, the names of all of us, which is why I hate thinking it has to end. Ever.

Then Smitty comes.

"Wait, don't tell me, let me guess," he shouts from the doorway. "I got it. You won!" It's his usual. He's looking right at me, and I'm embarrassed, caught dreaming about myself. Then I see I'm standing close next to Edwards, who Smitty considers a crud and a phony, which makes me afraid he classes me with him. The thing is, I admire the both of them.

Smitty steps just inside, into the fanned dark cool, hands on hips, sneering at everything with his stance. He snickers at me, at all of us, at softball games and the victories we celebrate with beer.

From behind him and round him the losing team players filed in now, circles of sweat under their arms, ovals on their chests and backs making their purple jerseys even darker. Hide-Away Bar. We took them 14-0 in seven innings. Their dirty spikes click on the tile floor and leave a trail of bits of grass and dried mud. In contrast to us as we mill at the bar, like sweated horses walking off the heat to keep muscles loose, waiting for the first foamy glasses of beer, Smitty stands still and apart, wearing a colorful flowing aloha shirt hanging out over pressed but faded slacks. He smiles and shows his gold-flecked teeth.

The losing captain, hauling out his sponsor's money to pay Les for the beer, looked at Smitty, then at me, puzzled to see a Negro in this neighborhood.

"RayBotts," Schneider said, "mark your glasses, the leech is here."

"He's the closest thing to a mascot for us since Les's pig died," Ray Botts said, pushing foam off the top of a glass with a wooden tongue depressor.

"Tee-bow," Smitty said, smiling at me, "your father work?"

"Nope," I obliged, "he's a cop." He came up to me at the bar, winked, lifted one finger to Ray Botts to include himself in on beer now being drawn, clear and yellow, in heavy pitchers. Les shoved a glass to him.

"Aaaagh?" Smitty said, rolling his lips dry of beer foam, grinning with his eyes at me. "If you didn't keep on winning, chum, I don't wonder but what I'd have to go to work in order to keep on drinking." Which is exactly what I often thought about myself when the first one was going down. I glowed, felt close to him.

He was a part of what we had there at Axel's Inn, and I wanted to keep him a part of it as much as I wanted to keep Edwards, or Ray Botts, Voss, Schneider, Les, all of us.

The first year we took the county championship—that year we got as far as the state sectionals—we came pouring in out of the sun to drink winner's beer, and there he was. Smitty was at the far end of the bar, smoking a cigarette he must have mooched from Les, chewing cashews from a cellophane sack, nursing a bottled beer. I watched, and he stayed, watching; when the barrel was down below half, most of the losing team gone, nobody to care, Ray Botts handed a glass to Smitty and told him to suck up, it was free.

He came every Saturday after that, arriving just after we'd get back from the Pumping Station to celebrate, probably coming all the way across town from the Negro district to cadge free beer. But not without integrity. Not obliging. I noticed.

He never cringed, never crab-walked sideways up to the bar. He never had to ask for a glass, and I never heard him say thanks for a drop, for anything. And when the Saturday got dark outside, the noise over, the sweat dried and stiff in our jerseys, the half-dozen or so of us left drew up at a table with Smitty. What he did, what he contributed—I doubt he ever so much as held a softball or a bat in his hands—he talked. Just talked. He mocked, needled one or all of us. He told stories, jokes, lies. It's what he did, he said, for a living, being as he never worked, as a matter of pride. He could talk.

As for instance. Once he told us about his ten-dollar smile, the one he used to borrow ten dollars with. Later the same afternoon he borrowed ten dollars from Ray Botts, only reminding us what he'd done after he had the tenner in hand. Ray Botts chased him around the bumper pool table and out the door, but we needled him so hard, all got to laughing, he let Smitty back inside.

And that's what got to me, bothered me, started me sour. His talk. The time half a dozen men and their women came in after a matinee at the Repertory Theater across the street. Les told them he didn't have the makings for Old Fashioneds and Whiskey Sours, but they settled for booze and mix. Ray Botts started the hassle. One of the men, tuxedo jacket and all, turned to his woman and said, "Look at the team."

"Ooew," Ray Botts said loudly, turning to Fred Jantke, drawing his mouth out in a pucker, "Ah dew wish ah had gone to the thee-ahtah this ahft-tah-noon, doe-wen't yew?" The man turned around to face us, rotated his glass on the bar with two thick fingers. Les the regular bartender looked hard at Ray Botts. Fred Jantke's no fighter that I ever knew, but he was beer-tight enough to oblige: "Rah-lay," he said, "ah dew think the theah-tah is grand!"

The man in the tuxedo jacket ran his tongue over his lips and looked us over one by one to see how many were ready to back up our boy. I dropped my eyes—George Thibault is no fighter I can assure you—and discarded the comment I was rehearsing. I stared into my beer, drank deep.

Fred Jantke stood up, cupped one hand to his mouth, pointed to the tuxedo man, and sang out, "Ollie ollie oxen all free, this guy's lookin' bad at me!" I ducked automatically and shoved my chair back to get running room; Smitty sneered at the whole thing and lit up a cigarette mooched from my pack on the table.

That tuxedo guy seemed to stumble, he came so fast. He grabbed Fred Jantke where he stood, handful of jersey, and cocked a punch while bulling him back into the bar. Ray Botts picked up a free chair to crown him with. It could have been right nasty.

It was a miracle, Schneider walking in just then. "Drop the chair, Ray," he said. I was seeing him rest the heel of his hand on the leaded billy he carried in a loop on his cartridge belt, just in front of his service .38.

"Tell this crud to go to the Mint Bar then, this ain't no cocktail lounge!" Ray Botts screamed. But he dropped the lumber. Tuxedo man let loose Fred Jantke's jersey and wiped his hand on his sleeve.

"You started it, RayBotts, admit it," Les said, mostly to Schneider. Schneider made Ray Botts and Fred Jantke leave, talked to Les and the tuxedo people for a second, downed a courtesy shot from Les, nodded hello to Smitty and me on his way out. I don't clown near so often around him since then.

"He sure as hell handled that nice," I said to Smitty.

Smitty wrinkled his nose, showed his inlays, tossed off his beer, said, "Would have served them right if he pinched them for it." Then he went up to the bar to refill our pitcher.

"What the hell," I said when he came back, "are you siding with those people against RayBotts?" The possibility shook me. Smitty was supposed to be one of us. I tried to hold onto it, the games we won, our celebration, that gold above the bar, I felt my glow fade.

Smitty laughed. "Tee-bow," he said, helping himself to my cigs again, "I'll tell you something you already know. Ray Botts is a bully. So is Jantke. Neither one's tough, but they got to believe they're bad actors just to live with themselves. Trouble is they get so much beer in them, they know better. Then they need somebody like my man in the suit. And baseball games, and all that kind of crap."

That hurt. "You wouldn't have helped them?" I glanced at the row of trophies over Les's head.

"I'd done just like the man, Tee-bow, tied into the both of them—"

"Either one could cream you easy," I said. No lie. Smitty is maybe five-seven at most, skinnier than me and not near as straight.

"So what?" he said. "Thing is, next time they'd bully somebody else, wouldn't they. Two kinds of people can't take me, Tee-bow. Phonies and bad actors. Phonies because they can't take anyone knows the truth about them, bullies 'cause they only bully people who don't fight back."

Now that was the beginning, when I started losing my moments. They still came, came when I stood out in right field at the Pumping Station and answered the infield chatter with my own pepper, when I dug my spikes in at the plate and took my practice cuts right up to the second the ball left the mound, when we poured sweating into

Axel's and huddled up under that row of gold trophies to wait for the barrel to be tapped. But I couldn't stay away from Smitty, because I know the truth when I hear it as good as the next man, even when I was dreaming to myself about how my name was going to be up there forever and ever.

This Saturday, this day it happened, Edwards and Les and Schneider were talking just generally, Edwards telling Schneider about the examination he passed for police academy. "Tee-bow," Smitty said, "cigarette me." I slid my pack down the bar to him and settled in to listen to Edwards. Now he was telling the story again about having known No-Hit Don Larsen of the New York Yankees. "Schneider," he said, "I know Don Larsen very well, played ball with him, and Don said when he signed with the Yankees they took him into the locker room at Yankee Stadium, and they showed him where Ruth had his locker, and they said to him now you're a Yankee. . . ." He told it often, but with enough beer nobody cared. Some of us maybe even believed him.

"When the hell you going to get a job, Tee-bow?" Smitty asks me.

"I got a job."

"Name it."

"Encyclopedia salesman." Partly true, since I'd only recently been canned from that. Smitty laughed.

"I mean a real job."

"Same day you get one."

"That's different," he said. "I know I'm a bum and I don't care, but you do. So when you going to work?" Players from both teams were settling down at tables now to play Sheepshead, which is how Voss supplements his unemployment compensation. The fast drinking was over, the steady strong drinking on the way. Going sour. I ignored Smitty.

Les and Schneider were looking down at Edwards' right arm, which he had laid out, palm up, on the bar like a cut of meat. Edwards looked at his arm with this look, like thinking, could it be true this was really his very own arm? Schneider and Les looked respectful, quiet, like they'd look at somebody's bankroll.

"A million-dollar arm!" Edwards said, shaking his pink head. "A million dollars, and I threw it out on American Legion doubleheaders and fastpitch for beer." Les and Schneider lifted their eyes in sympathy. What we all understood was that nobody was called on to say anything.

"You're a liar," Smitty said, grinning over his free beer, "and a pennywink. You eat cat shit and your breath stinks." Les hustled away to help Ray Botts draw beer. Schneider adjusted his hat and hitched up his cartridge belt, groaning faintly. I watched. Edwards' face showed the shock, as good as if Smitty'd picked up the sunburned arm and thrown it at him. Smitty kept his eyes steady on him, smiling his you're-a-liar-and-I-know-it smile, with the gold-rimmed edges of his lower teeth showing, the mooched cigarette burning slowly between his brown fingers, the beer glass beading in his other hand.

"You suppose they'll pressure you to pitch for the police department after you start, Big Ed?" I said, just to be saying something.

"May be," he said. He dropped his eyes and walked away from Smitty's laugh to a table where someone asked him did he strike out thirteen or fourteen today.

"You have to do that?" I said.

"What's he to you that you got to wet-nurse him?" Smitty said.

"That isn't it at all, man. What is it with you? You get a kick out of calling people liars and bums and all?"

"But ain't it the damn truth?" he said, and shook another cigarette out of my pack.

"Look at you," I said. "Goddamn leech, sponge my weeds, sponge beer, sponge—"

"Do I deny it?"

"What the hell's that matter!" I yelled. "I sweated two hours in the sun for this beer at least, so did Edwards and the rest of us, you come in, drink up for nothing, and give us your smart mouth to boot —you bastard, Smitty—"

"Tee-bow!" he said so loud I shut up. "How long are you gonna kid yourself this is all a big deal?" He opened his hand and stretched his arm to include everything, the players standing around Ray Botts to get their pitchers filled, the Sheepshead game at the table, Les wiping the bar, everything. The pool table, the jukebox. The trophies.

"What do you know about it," I said. I spoke softly now. "What do you know, leeching crud? See that county league trophy? This season's over, you're gonna see my name up there. All of us, our names up there. Stick in your hat how much you know about it, sponger." He laughed.

"Maybe when you're forty they'll let you be a big-time manager like Ray, huh?" I looked at Ray Botts, the bully, working over the barrel. His paunch hung over his belt. He was balder every time I met him. He was telling someone about a fastpitch team upstate that would doubtless be invited to the regionals . . . but they had no pitching, he was saying with confidence.

Schneider left to finish his beat. The married men left. The men who worked graveyard shift left. It got down to one table of us, Voss playing solitaire, Ray Botts talking about his ideas for publicity when we got our bid to the state invitational this year.

"Soon as we get the official letter," he said, "I'm calling the newspapers and I'm getting those jokers to give us some coverage. Hell, the rest of the entries are big, right? Resort teams with college ringers, like we lost to in the sectionals last year. Hell, we're the only neighborhood tav-ren team's ever been invited two years running—three years with this year."

"Can you see the sports page put Axel's Inn in big print, RayBotts, though?" Voss said. He practiced palming cards. Me, I couldn't listen to that bar talk any more. I watched Smitty and Edwards.

"Didn't you ever fail at anything?" he asked Smitty.

"Plenty of times. Except I never lied about failing at anything is the difference."

"Listen, Smith," he said. He laid his arm out in front of him, clenched his fingers into a fist.

"Why the hell shouldn't we get the same publicity some smelly factory team loaded with ringers gets?" Ray Botts was saying.

Then Smitty called him a liar again, a liar and a eee-lapper. Edwards slapped his mouth. Ray Botts was suddenly hollering about the sink in the men's toilet. Smitty never flinched.

"You want to prove it?" he said.

"Damn right," Edwards said. He got up, a head and a half taller than Smith, seventy pounds heavier easy. Then everyone in the tavern knew what was up, and all the noise was over. In a second, I could see whose side everyone was on. It figured. They needed that state invitational, the mention on the sports page, the names engraved on the trophy. Like me.

"Kick his ass out, Les," Fred Jantke said, "he's got nothing to do with this place. He's a crud drinks free beer."

"You want me to handle your light work, Big Ed?" Ray Botts said, getting up now also.

Smitty put them down. He stood there with that ten-dollar, you're-a-damn-liar smile on his face. "Not in here you don't," Les said. He picked up the cue from the bumper pool table for authority.

"Come on out?" Smitty said to Edwards.

They headed for the door, and I was right behind them. Ray Botts moved too, but I turned on him and shouted in his face, "Yes, goddamn, I washed my funky hands in the sink! Clean it up and shut your damn lip about it!" And by God, he did. Stopped, I mean. Nobody came after us. We stood on the sidewalk in front of the tavern in the dusk. An air conditioner in the window of Les's upstairs apartment hummed and rattled.

When Edwards spoke, I finally understood. "He goes inside," he said, jerking a thumb at me. "Just you and me."

"I'm staying," I said, deciding that if Edwards whipped him—*when* he whipped him—I'd take a turn, lousy fighter that I am and always will be.

"Start something," Edwards said, sagging a little.

"Hobo your way over," Smitty said. "I'll pay your freight back." They mixed and traded punches. Three, maybe four, but I couldn't see exactly, only that it was about an even exchange, no marks on anybody. Just huffs of breath, a quick *thud thud* of sound, and then Smitty slipped, pushed not hit, into the gutter. He struggled to get his footing, and I figured Edwards would catch him off balance there and cream him.

But Edwards quit. He stood high over Smitty on the curb, sagging, put out his hand. "Let's shake, forget it," he whispered like he didn't want me to hear.

Smitty's aloha shirt was pulled open. He took time now to button it, wide open if Edwards laid into him. "Shake?" he said. "Not no, but hell no! Go on," he said, "hit me now while I'm fixing my shirt, hit me when my hands are down."

"Come on, Smitty," Edwards said, voice pleading, "shake and forget it."

"Afraid to hit me now, Big Ed? You afraid I'll get my sandwich while you're having a meal? Admit you're afraid and I'll shake with you, big man." Edwards pulled his hand back and stepped away from the gutter before he spoke.

"You little nigger," he said.

"Is that all you got left, Edwards?" is all Smitty said. Edwards turned around, looked down the street like he needed someplace to crawl in, away from everything. But the tavern was all there was. He walked in Axel's, the neon shining on his forehead. "Tell 'em all about it, Big Ed!" Smitty yelled after him.

"That's good enough," I said to him, "you said it enough. He knows. We all know."

"Did you see that, Tee-bow?" he said, smiling.

"I seen it." There must be something to it, I thought, if you can stand up to a man twice your size. Then I remembered how I was ready to take Edwards myself. "Come on," I said, "come on across the street, I'll buy you a beer at the Mint Bar." He winked and made a circle with his thumb and forefinger. "One sec," I said, "I need to get my mitt first."

I went in and picked up my glove from a booth. I didn't see Edwards. Nobody said anything until I was on the way out. "Practice, Tee-bow," Ray Botts said, "Wednesday, six-thirty, Pumping Station, practice."

"If I can make it," I said. "I don't know yet what I'm doing Wednesday." Smitty and I crossed the empty street.

"Make it two," he said. "That's the theater-in-the-round crowd. I never go there unless I got a firm promise of at least two drinks. They don't like serving Ni-grows, so I need two to take the trouble." I laughed with him.

"You come all the way across town for that, don't you, Smitty."

"Why not," he said. "It's my right, isn't it?"

"You're on," I said. I hold the door open for him, follow him inside to buy him a little victory beer. I am glowing.

Cemetery in Winter

She had been to the cemetery, my sister wrote me, and our mother's grave now looked the way any grave does; the rectangle of bare dirt was sodded in and the marker we ordered was in place. I could see it for myself next time I came back to Milwaukee for a visit. I don't remember if I wrote back that I was glad to hear that, or even if I mentioned it at all in my answer. My sister and I do not write often, but we never fail to answer each other's letters.

Mother never forgot her graves, so I felt I ought not to forget hers. Her dead were all in a family plot in Hambro, Illinois, the last buried, the plot filled when her father, my Grandfather Engstrom, died in 1938. I was only a year old then. But the dead, for her, were not dead, buried, forgotten. In her correspondence with girlhood friends who still lived in Hambro, she asked from to time if the cemetery custodians were living up to the contract providing perpetual care.

In summers, every two or three years, she took me with her on the nearly 300 mile Greyhound bus trip from Milwaukee to visit her friends, and her graves. I sat quietly on the screened porches with a glass of tepid lemonade or iced tea. Across wide parched lawns the heat rays rose from the streets of softened tar. I was bored, unable to follow the conversations my mother had with her friends from Hambro Township, Class of 1915, who had never married but stayed on in Hambro to teach or care for their parents, or who married the local Swedish farmboys and storekeepers and carpenters. One I remember was Hazel Larsen. She married Hambro's only doctor.

And someone, a retired Swedish farmboy, perhaps the good doctor himself, when office hours were over, drove us to the cemetery. I walked around the family plot behind my mother, very careful not to step on the graves of the Boom family, or the Berntsons', or Svanoes', or Nelsens', whose dead surrounded all that remained of those who bore the name Engstrom and came together to America in 1883 from Dalarna province in Sweden to find a better life.

Because it was so hot we stood in the shade of a tree. Yes, there were trees in the cemetery, some older than the graves, and the ground there was swollen by hard winter frosts that tipped the fading tombstones. My mother bent over until her head was next to mine, pointed where lay her father and mother, uncles Knute and Anton, their wives, Annie (for whom she was named) and Karin, her aunts Ida and Marie (they were my great-aunts, she told me; I had never known them) with their husbands, Elmer and Joe.

She told me little stories about each of them, but it was too hot to listen. I played games: subtracting birth dates from dates of death to see how old they lived to be (1872 from 1936 is how much?), and I have forgotten the stories and I regret it. But she knew them, she knew them all and never forgot.

Then the retired Swedish farmboy or the good doctor and his wife led the way back to his car at the cemetery entrance, where my mother stopped to let the custodial supervisor know she had been there in case he was the sort who would get lax about keeping the graves up. I picked my way carefully behind them, avoiding the gentle mounds of grass covering Peggy Boom, Sonia Svanoe, and Aanen Nelson (1856 to 1923; he lived to be sixty-seven). There were trees to shade the tombstones and gravel paths, and wild flowers and natural shrubs left undisturbed between the plots.

It was winter, before Christmas, the first time I returned to Milwaukee after her death. There had been snow early in November, but it melted and there were bare streets and sidewalks. Then it snowed more than four inches, and it turned very cold. I had nearly reached the cemetery before the car was warm enough to turn the heater on.

There were changes already. An enormous Treasure Island store, a discount house that sold everything, hawking its name in signs high and large enough to read for blocks, was open for business next to the cemetery. It had been a skeleton of concrete, unfleshed by neon and plastic and glass the day of my mother's funeral, the summer before. At the wide iron scroll-work gate to the cemetery, an enterprising florist had opened a jerrybuilt greenhouse on the other side of the road to sell sprays and wreaths for the graves, his prices chalked on blackboards at the shoulder of the road.

Under the fresh snow the only landmark inside the gates was the huge chapel that could be rented for funerals. My sister had been inside it the day she came to see that the marker was in place. One entire wing, she had written, contained wall-high banks of mausoleum vaults, another sealed niches to hold the urns of the cremated. Organ music played continually inside, and the moment dusk fell, floodlights concealed in flower beds illuminated the clean stone walls. There was an office there also, and no doubt they had a chart of the cemetery, like the diagrams of seats available for dramas and baseball games displayed in ticket offices; I could have stopped to ask directions, but didn't.

The macadam drive made a circle in front of the chapel, and I turned off to the right. I knew, I remembered, my mother was buried to the right of the chapel, some distance away. There were little metal signs along the drive giving the lot numbers, A-3 and A-4, but I could not remember if my sister had written the lot number to me or not. The only trees were along the inside of the fence, and a few near the chapel, new young trees in their first winter, tied with strips of cloth to stakes driven next to them to support them against the wind. I looked for a certain large bush; there had been an even, high bush, like a windbreak, at the edge of the drive where our funeral procession stopped. I remember walking past it behind the pallbearers, my eyes on the grass, where I saw the flat tracks left by the machine that dug the grave, but there were many bushes, all stripped and shrunk now in winter.

From the drive, the lots were flat and white. This cemetery has no stones, only flush bronze markers, because it is cheaper that way and the grass can be mowed in wide, economical swaths. Here and there were clumps of flowers and wreaths, black against the snow, and a few little flags stuck over the graves of war veterans.

The drive curves, and it seemed there was a curve I remembered at the funeral procession, and finally I stopped there and got out and threw away my cigarette. I walked back to the nearest stunted bush and left the drive. I tried to walk the same distance as before, but when I reached a point that seemed far enough, there were only my footprints in from the drive behind me. The flush bronze markers were visible in outline beneath the snow, but names and dates could not be read. I stood there until the wind made my eyes tear, and then I saw two older women watching me from another plot farther in, on the other side of another branch of the drive.

I bent over and brushed the snow off a marker with my glove. The man's name was Bostwick. He lived forty-eight years. I could have gone back to the office in the chapel. I could have pretended that Bostwick belonged to me in order to satisfy the curiosity of the old women watching me. I could have gone without finding my mother's grave if I had not known my sister would ask me if I had been there, if I did not feel the memory of my mother and her loyalty to her dead made it impossible.

I tried a few more there. One after another, stepping sideways without straightening up, I wiped snow from the markers. A woman named Candon, and her husband, dead in the same year. Jurina, aged sixty-one; I knew a Jurina somewhere once, college, the army perhaps. An unpronounceable Pole, a family marker with space left for the still-living children, though their given names and dates of birth were cut in bronze already. A man who had once been a corporal and served in a regiment of the Red Arrow division, his marker provided by the government.

When I stood up I was breathing hard. My nose ran. My fingers and toes and ears no longer felt the cold. I walked across the plot, stepping over the outlines of the markers toward the old women, who were talking now, no longer watching me.

I walked up close to them as if I were going to ask them directions, but stopped when they looked at me and moved away from me and away from each other. They visited different graves, went their respective ways now, as if they met here often to gossip and trade in memories. One worked, taking the snow away from her marker with a whisk broom she had in her pocket, propping the weathered wreath until it was just so, standing back to see if it was right. The other simply stood with one foot in front of the other, her chin buried in her scarf, as if meditating, preparing to communicate.

When I saw they would not speak to me I bent again and cleared the snow away. I do not remember all the names. Some were only names and dates, some said *Beloved Husband* or *Dearest Daughter*, some were adorned with scrolls and bronze flowers and angels with their cheeks puffed out blowing on trumpets. I uncovered the markers at random; I used a system, lining up with the bell tower of the chapel and the evenly spaced shrubs at the edge of the drive. I took off my gloves and blew on my hands to warm them, kicked at the snow with my wet shoes. I read the names, and then I stopped reading them, seeing no names or dates until I found what I was looking for.

When I found it there was nothing except a name that was my name and the dates of my mother's sixty-six years, there on the marker like all the other markers I had seen. I was on my knees then, moving between two rows of graves. I found my mother's and I got up and brushed the snow off me. I looked around and saw the women leaving, arm in arm. I stayed a short while and then left.

I read her name several times to myself, and then aloud because there was no one to hear me. But it was too cold, or perhaps it had taken too long. I read it and tried to remember things, but there was only a bronze marker like all the others, and the snow, the little trees held up with rags and stakes near the fence, the dull white chapel off behind me. I went back to the car, retracing the patches of rectangular bronze I had bared to reflect the sun, and I lit a cigarette in the car for warmth before I drove away.

Had I gone to see Mother's grave? my sister asked me that evening. I said yes, I had, and that's all we said about it. When we see each other I know we both want to talk about her, recall things she said or did when we were small. But we don't, usually. We remember, but we do not usually speak of what we remember.

When Times Sit In

It was Clontine, the Red Fox, who first brought the dark specter of Times into Jay Fair's consciousness. The two men had been talking in front of Brown's Shine Parlor and Leather Products, and Jay Fair had started toward his Impala convertible at the curb when Clontine spoke to him of Times. It was not that Jay Fair did not know of Times, but only that this mention forced the image before him and spoiled what had been a cheerful and free outlook on the warm late summer afternoon.

"You cool now, Jay Fair," said Clontine, "but you never know when Times be right behind you, smilin' and grinnin' and just waitin' to sit in and make you low."

Jay Fair stopped and turned around to face the man whose hair color made most of the boys refer to him as Red Fox behind his back. His brow creased in puzzlement, as though the name of Times had caused him an inexplicable chill.

"No, mon, no," Jay Fair said, brushing the cold, dark hint of Times away from some dusky corner of his mind. "Times don't be lookin' for no Jay Fair. Jay Fair be cool always, and his coins be too long for old Times to be sittin' in, mon."

Clontine turned away to go into Brown's as he threw over his shoulder, "Just when you think you at you best, that be when Times get on you and beat you down so low you don't have enough to buy a coke, and you be over in line for turkey-neck at the Baptist Church."

"Aw, mon, no," Jay Fair said, dismissing Times and Clontine

both. He held his arm close to his side, spreading out his hand and waggling his palm, saying "Be cool, mon, be cool, don't hurt yourself none."

"I see you, man," Clontine said.

"I gone soak over to Joe Harris' and play me a little number . . . just like I do if Times come too close," Jay Fair fired as a parting shot. But Clontine had disappeared into Brown's and had not heard him.

Jay Fair slid across the hot leather upholstery of the Impala and ensconced himself behind the wheel. No, no mon, Times don't be lookin' for no Jay Fair.

But that image, that picture of Times was somehow too clear in his mind's eye. Incredibly, he shuddered in the heat from a flash he had that Times might be walking up the street even now, hoping to catch him unaware, perhaps slide in beside him in the Impala and go riding about the streets with him.

No, mon no, damn no! Jay Fair roared away from the curb, instantly relieved. Times had been left somewhere behind, and besides, he was always too cool.

He drove vaguely in the direction of Joe Harris', but to impress upon himself the very concreteness of his immunity to Times, he made several detours to pass by the corners where he knew some boys would be loitering. He passed them slowly, with his radio playing loudly.

"Hey, man, Jay Fair, you got some tough sounds!" they yelled.

"My man!" they said with a wave.

Jay Fair dipped his head only slightly in their direction. He let his arm hang down over the side of the Impala, and just as he passed closest to a group of his men, he waggled his palm and said, "Be cool, be cool, don't hurt yourself none," in a controlled voice that could barely be heard.

No, mon, no, Times don't be nowheres near Jay Fair. Jay Fair be the man that Times don't get, don't never get. No, Times could not touch, must never touch him. And if Times should ever sit in, if Times should ever grin and smile, and make Jay Fair low, he must never admit it. He must fight Times off and never, never even to himself, admit it. Jay Fair pressed down on the accelerator pedal, and the Impala's tail pipes chuckled for him as he headed toward Joe Harris' in haste to play a number, sure he would hit one.

"My man! Jay Fair!" Joe Harris said happily when he walked in.

"Say, Jay Fair," said another man who was about to begin a game of nine ball.

"Be cool, be cool," Jay Fair answered with his waggling palm.

"What you need, Jay Fair?" Joe Harris asked.

"My coins be shortin' up just a little, so I figure I maybe play a few small numbers, mon."

"Yeah, Jay Fair, play a number and see can we keep old Times off us, huh?" Joe Harris said as he walked behind the bar to get a policy slip.

Like a foggy shroud, Jay Fair felt Times near him, frightening him terribly. "Goddamn, mon, ain't nobody ask you to tell me none about Times! Goddamn, if you be jivin' me all the time when I come in here, I go somewheres else for a number and you don't never see no Jay Fair in here!" He slammed his fist down on the bar in front of Joe Harris, almost ready for violence.

"Easy, man, easy, you know I'm okay, you know how I pay off when you win." The man at the pool table looked with curiosity at Jay Fair, who was sorry now that he had shouted. But the reference to Times had struck home like the sound of a coffin being nailed shut, coming so soon after Clontine, and his money was getting just a little short.

He had intended to play only one number, maybe two, but now he panicked just a bit. "I play about three for three," he said. He removed nine dollars from his gold clip and gave them to Joe Harris. Jay Fair had not had a dream for several days, so he picked his numbers at random. He waited impatiently for Joe Harris to fill out the slips, wanting to be back out in the sun with his Impala, for it seemed darker and unfriendly in the pool hall now, almost cold.

"Be cool," he said quietly as he left.

He drove about the streets again, waving to boys that he knew, basking in their respectful recognition of him, but he could not shake Times' shade. He passed two men sweeping the gutter on a relief project, and he could imagine Times pointing to them, saying to him: *See there, Jay Fair, that's what I'm gone do to you. I'm gone sit in and take away all you coins, and you be so low when winter come you don't have enough to buy you a coke,* the voice rolling like the fall of cold, black clods of frozen earth.

No, mon, damn Times, damn winter, damn no turkey-neck soup, mon, Jay Fair be cool always, and no Times and no nothin' be sittin' in on him! No, not to him, not to no Jay Fair that don't happen. There be plenty boys for old Times, he don't be needin' no Jay Fair.

And though Jay Fair cruised the streets and waved to his boys, and though he could feel the solidness of his security in the strong whine of the Impala, he could not evade the shadow of Times. Finally, in a desperate attempt to quiet his fear, he drove to his sister's house.

"Jay Fair," she said, "what you gettin' all dressed for?"

"Jay Fair be goin' to Celebrity Night at the Bronzeville and soak a while," he answered. He had put on his finest summer suit, shaved and trimmed his thin moustache.

"You always be so clean," his sister said in admiration.

"Jay Fair be cool always," he said with pride. He had given himself a hair process too, and it lay smooth and bright as soft, black leather. He knotted a gold tie and thought of how far the long knife of Times must be from him now.

Jay Fair, you wig be leapin' and you creases be all clean . . . you got a big tough diamond ring, and you wheels be mean. He laughed. Mon, if old Times creep around, I be specializin' in rhymin' up a few small items on him, and just read old Times off. "Jay Fair!" he sang, "you much too young a man to have so many women!" He grabbed his sister and danced her laughingly around the room.

The band was swinging when he walked into the Bronzeville, but the leader made a special welcome for him with a dip of his horn. Jay Fair said nothing, only waggled his palm in return. He took a table to one side, ordering a drink, but ignoring it to tap out the numbers the band played. Several women smiled to him from the bar, but he only tacitly recognized them; sometimes with a raised eyebrow of skepticism, sometimes with a wry expression of disbelief and disdain. He was cool always.

Later, when Jay Fair was a little intoxicated, the band leader put the spotlight on him and said to the crowd, after a roll of the trap drum, "I see we have one local celebrity here who I hope will oblige us by doing a number for us." The crowd, most of whom knew him, and knew that he was always cool, stomped and whistled.

"Hey, my man, come on, give us one number!"

"Hey you, you Jay Fair, sing one man!"

Jay Fair smirked only slightly and looked down at his drink. "Naw, mon, naw," he whispered.

"What say, Jay Fair?" the band leader said. "Let's give the man a hand and see will he sing one for us," he called to the crowd. The crowd clapped loudly, then louder, as Jay Fair stood up reluctantly and ambled toward the bandstand. All the way across the floor he waggled both his palms and softly said, "Be cool, be cool."

He started off with "Traveling Man," which got such a hand that he did "Annie Had a Baby" and "Long John" too before he did a small step and hopped lightly off the bandstand and ambled to his table with the spotlight following him, saying "Be cool, be cool" all the way back.

No, old ghost Times don't be no place near the Bronzeville tonight. Times out in the street, prowlin' around all cold and hungry, but Jay Fair be sittin' in at the Bronzeville, too cool, always too cool.

The singing and the applause, and perhaps the few drinks had mellowed him a little; they had really made him feel secure. Never had he felt quite so fine and safe, so immortal. He decided to really do it right, really get a feeling so far away from Times that he might never have to think of it again, ever.

Jay Fair called over to one of the girls at the bar, the lightest and prettiest one in the Bronzeville. "Lee, hey Lee baby, come sit by Jay Fair and have a small nip." She came over quickly, and he had the waitress pour a half-pint of Ancient Age up for two. Then he called over the man who took Polaroid pictures. He put his arm around the girl and they raised their glasses in a toast to whoever might look at the photo someday, and the man snapped them.

Many times in the future, Jay Fair would look at the photo and still not believe in it. Everything in it was so cool. The woman is the lightest and prettiest. His wig is leaping, and the baronial crest on the left breast of his fine summer jacket is distinct. The label on the Ancient Age can be read, and on the hand that holds his glass, Jay Fair's diamond looks big.

But somewhere, either to the left or the right of the picture, Times must have been watching. Just at that very moment, Jay Fair thought, when the man was taking the picture, old Times must have slipped up from somewhere near the bar, silent as an undertaker, and cast the mould of his leer over Jay Fair and his light, pretty woman. Just when he felt the best, when he felt sure that Times was locked out of the Bronzeville like the plague, and out of his life forever, he must have been smiling on him, ready to sit in.

Times waited. The good safe feeling lasted for a while. The band leader motioned him over, and they went into the men's room and smoked some stuff. When he was quite mellow, Jay Fair went back to the woman and told her that he would look her up sometime.

"Hey, my man, Jay Fair," someone at the bar shouted after him, "you goin' already?"

"Be cool, mon, be cool," Jay Fair said with his hands. There were more friendly words from the bar for him that echoed happily over the dark sidewalk when he was outside, and their warmth aided Jay Fair in feeling that he walked at least a foot above the pavement, despite the slightly sobering effect of the chill night air.

Times was gone, the chance of hitting a number on Joe Harris' wheel, the applause of the crowd for his singing, all gone, and only the dream-walk a foot above the pavement.

He slid behind the wheel of the Impala. No, mon, no, Jay Fair be always cool. Always and always. It was cold, but then summer was nearly over, and damn winter anyhow! Near him, if he had not smoked, and if he were not mellow on the Ancient Age, he would have felt the bony movements of Times. But as Clontine said, Times would sit in only when Jay Fair had forgotten all about him; then Times would be looking for him.

He slapped the Impala into gear, and cramping the wheel hard, he jumped the car into the middle of the street and directly into the path of a Buick coming up behind.

There was an impact that threw him up against the wheel, bumping him up against the windshield, and a tin-sounding crackle and crumple of the rear end of the Impala mashing in. Jay Fair was jarred to his senses, coming down that one foot of air cushion to walk on the pavement like all mortal men, and he perceived the hand and the skull-smile of Times in what had happened.

He tried to talk to the big man from the Buick. "Look, mon, let's be cool in this. You car still move, so you just drive away, and you send me the bill for whatever you be needin', and we don't need no police or nothin' on this."

"No, hell no," the big man said excitedly, "we've got to call an officer and make a report, I have to make a report for my insurance."

Jay Fair pleaded with him, almost crying, but the man seemed completely unconcerned with what this would mean for Jay Fair, who owed money on the wrecked Impala and had not bothered with insurance.

"Mon," he said, "I got to get me out of this, I can't be havin' no trouble now."

"Look, I'm not going to argue with you, I'm going to call a squad and you can talk to the police about. . . ."

No, the man would not listen, and in his relentless, non-pitying attitude of unconcern, Jay Fair imagined the cruel laughter of Times. Perhaps he thought that Times had come to rest, gleefully, on the big man's shoulder, or maybe he even thought that the big man was Times.

But it was more of a last, diehard swing of protest against the senseless unfairness of Times that Jay Fair felt as he lashed out with his best punch, a bolo right, catching the man neatly under the chin, sprawling him on the street. The man's wife screamed from inside the Buick.

The big man got up and went into a professional crouch, and Jay Fair forgot the frustration of fighting against Times and reverted to his cool fighting self. Maybe I got me a real dick-head here, he thought, maybe he gone nothin' but lay some strong wood on me.

No, the man had nothing; Jay Fair caught him once, twice, three times, a small combination that he had learned well and practiced hard, and the man sprawled limply in the street again. Come on again, mon, for Jay Fair be rhymin' you up and readin' you off, and layin' some bad, bad wood on you ugly head!

By then there were people from the Bronzeville watching, and a policeman grabbed Jay Fair's arm. He turned and hit the policeman, staggering him. Then he knew it was Times, hearing the voice of falling earth. *I gone take you, Jay Fair, gone take you and bury you so*

you don't be able to buy you a coke, yeah, gone take you, Jay Fair!
Times closing in on him. Come and get it, you! Come and get you
wood from Jay Fair, who be too cool always for you, come and he
stick a whole mess of lef' hooks on you! The policeman arched his
nightstick high and hit Jay Fair only medium hard, and then
straddled him to cuff his hands behind his back.

"Lawyer Shulsky," Jay Fair said into the phone, "this be Jay Fair.
You come down here and be gettin' me loose. This don't be too cool,
mon, not hittin' on too much. They got me in the slam, mon."

When Lawyer Shulsky, whom Jay Fair had long ago engaged to
handle such items, had arrived to go bail for him, he asked to see his
client before doing anything.

"I'm gonna have to have some money, Jay, I'm just gonna have to
have something. You're in pretty deep, pretty serious this time. This
ain't no bastardy action, boy, you're in with the big boys now,
assault, drunken driving, resisting apprehension, boy, you're in
trouble."

"Mon, I don't be havin' too much," Jay Fair said weakly. "Times
got . . . I don't be too long on my coins, mon." No, mon, no, Jay Fair
don't be sayin' nothin' about Times, or you be so low you never get
up. No, not you, Jay Fair, you be cool always, you find a way, got to
be a way.

"I'll tell you what," Lawyer Shulsky said in his cigar wheeze, "you
give me that diamond and what money you got, and I'll see what I
can get for what's left of the car, and I'll see what I can do about
bail. You're gonna have to take care of the lien on the car your own
way, and this ain't got nothing to do with whatever you get sued for.
If you want help on that, or when you come to trial, I'm gonna have
to see some more money, okay?"

"Yeah, mon," Jay Fair said, removing his ring, "just be gettin' me
outta the slam."

When the bail was set, Jay Fair was released. He had expected to
be cheered by the open streets after the gloom of the lockup, but
there was a feeling of overcast to the outside also. Times, mon,
Times be anyplace huntin' you, very close now. Without a cent, he
waited until it was dark so that he could sneak to his sister's house.

"Jay Fair, I can't be havin' you around here when you don't bring no money into this house. You gonna have to leave your clothes here so I got somethin' if you wanna sleep here," his sister said.

As Times patiently waited for him, he made a final effort to escape from the end that he knew loomed for him, still unwilling to believe that it could happen to him. He took the metal comb and the oil and went to a different neighborhood, where few of the boys knew him, to make enough money for a last show. There was still a chance, he could take a couple of numbers at Joe Harris'; he might be right back there again, straight, cool.

"Hey, mon," Jay Fair said as the stranger walked by. He slouched in front of a tavern with the oil and the comb in a paper sack. "Mon, you wig don't be looking too swell, not too tough. Maybe I could be settin' it leapin' for you with a small process."

"How much you want?"

"Say five and no jive, mon." He could still rhyme up a few small items at will.

"You got a place?"

"No, mon, anywheres you say."

He stayed away from his sister's, for he was in disgrace there. He held on to his money until he had enough to make a payment at the credit clothiers, where he fitted himself with a new front of British-style clothes. One day he set his hair with a process and went to an auto dealer's, where he persuaded the salesman to let him have a Cadillac for a test drive.

He went slowly past Brown's Shine Parlor and Leather Products, where he knew the boys would be. For seventy feet he drove slowly, one arm hanging out, palm waggling, saying softly, "Be cool, be cool, don't hurt yourself none."

"Hey, Jay Fair, I see you soakin' in a new short."

"Jay Fair, when you get out of that slam?"

"You clean from head to toe, man, most cool."

He would have liked to stop, but he had to get the Cadillac back to the dealer and explain why he didn't want to buy it just now. Anyway, it steered harder than he was used to with the Impala.

It became harder for him to make any money, for he had worked that neighborhood over pretty well, and he did not dare to work his own neighborhood, for everyone would know then that Times . . . no, that he was low, that his coins were short. But there was a last chance for him, for survival, to be cool, if he could get to Joe Harris' and play a number, if he could get there without having to talk to any of the boys and answer questions, for if they still believed, then he could still believe.

To be safe, he put on his best and cleanest British-style front, the one with a gold tie and vest. He set his hair with a process, using the last of the oil, and walked to Joe Harris'. He had not eaten at all that day, and he could not afford a sandwich if he were to get a number, so he stopped in a grocery store and bought a small box of crackers to eat after he got his number.

"Say, mon, put that in a sack for me, huh?"

"That's nineteen cents."

Nineteen mon, cool, combinations of nineteen. No dream for many, many days; only vague memories of nightmares in which he smothered in total, confining darkness. But nineteen would do, it might be the thing.

He played his number, combinations of nineteen, but he had no real confidence in it. As he walked out of the pool room, he saw the Red Fox, Clontine, trot down the street toward him, calling to him, "My man! My man! My man Jay Fair!"

Damn Red Fox, never be cool, never will be cool, damn Red Fox.

"Hey, my man, you must have been in the slam somewhat long. Hey, where you Cadillac, Jay Fair? I hear you got you a Cadillac now."

"Aw, mon, it be in the garage now, I be havin' the steerin' fixed a little."

"Hey, Jay Fair, what you got in that old sack, man?"

"Be cool, be cool," Jay Fair said, pulling away from him, knowing it was all over, hearing the laughter and seeing the skull-smile, the hard, cruel smile of Times in the brisk air.

"What is it, Jay Fair?" he asked, grabbing the sack and opening it. "Crackers? Hey, crackers!"

"Okay, mon, I know it . . . I say it . . . Times got me, mon." The words came out final, hurting. Jay Fair felt the cold in his bones as Times sat in, felt it in the dead autumn leaves that were strewn over the sidewalk, felt it in the unbelieving, stupid laughter of Clontine the Red Fox, felt it in the first funereal rush of winter-promising air as he turned away to go to the Baptist Church and line up for turkey-neck soup.

Kiss in the Hand

My sister Phyllis is a tower of strength. "When I get to be that age," she said to me, "and start talking to the wall and wetting my pants, I hope somebody will be kind enough to slip me an overdose or nudge me in front of a truck." Phyllis, because she's strong, was the one who bore the burdens when our aunt died and there were so many things to be done. I came along to help just before the end, but then, what could I do?

She picked me up at the airport; I can remember trying to teach her to drive when I was sixteen and she was thirty-two. She handled that Chicago traffic like a cabdriver. "I'd rather see Mother dead ten years earlier than the way Aunt Margaret is, Buddy," she said to me.

"I still don't see why you catch all the responsibility."

"Sure it's responsibility. But the boys can't leave their jobs and their families, and I can." The *boys* are her sons. I have no family of my own. Phyllis is divorced. That's another proof of her strength, the way she raised those children alone, supported them, educated them, prospered. "Uncle Paul isn't any help. He doesn't always seem to know what's happening, or at least if he does know he doesn't realize what it means yet."

"I always think of Paul as one of the most precise men I ever met."

"He's seventy-four himself. My God," Phyllis said, "he's the one I always thought would go first, his ulcers and his blood pressure, his legs give out on him when he's walking. He doesn't dare to walk to the corner store; he could fall and break his skull."

"It doesn't seem fair. I mean what kind of a life is it when you live that long and end up like this?"

"Well it happens. And somebody's got to do what has to be done. Paul's steel pension and his social security are enough for Aunt Margaret's cost there. I don't imagine he'll like living with Jean, but he's got to be realistic too."

"What's an embolism?" I asked.

"It's a clot, obstruction of some kind that lodges in the brain. It's just a matter of time. She could live two hours or she could live ten years. The mind goes and eventually you're a vegetable. Sometimes she's rational and then in a minute she hardly knows you."

"You think she'll recognize me?"

"That's impossible to say, Buddy."

"I wish there was something I could do. Money or something. A magic wand is what I need."

"Well if she knows you it'll make her feel good to know you came to see her. That's all you can do." I doubt, seriously, that I could have made it that quickly driving the rush hour from O'Hare Field to Waukegan. She really can drive.

"Hello boy, hello Buddy boy, how are you boy," my Uncle Paul said as he shook my hand. We stopped at Jean's, his daughter's house, long enough to pick him up and take him along to the nursing home to see my aunt. I hadn't seen him for nearly a year. I thought at first he was going to weep, or had been weeping, then realized it was only that his eyes ran constantly. I had to shout for him to hear, and he'd become so frail the cord running from the hearing aid in his shirt pocket to his ear looked more like a piece of wire patching to keep him together. I had to keep a hand on his arm as we walked to the car, and I remembered how as a boy I used to flex my muscle for adults to feel.

"No good coming home any more, no good, is it, boy?" he said. I thought at first he referred to my mother's unexpected death a year before; he'd said that then, at her funeral.

"Phyllis says she's very comfortable at this home, Uncle Paul," I shouted at his good ear.

"No good," he said, "no home any more." My uncle had been

quite a man once. He'd been shipwrecked off Borneo, killed a man, another sailor, with a knife, saw two men hold a gunfight in a saloon in Texas, and that same time, in Texas, he shook hands with Francisco Madero. All this was long before he married my mother's sister, my Aunt Margaret.

It's as much as can be done," Phyllis said as she put the car in gear. She'd done everything. Jean and her husband seemed helpless. They tried to get her parents into a Masonic home first; Paul had been a Mason for thirty-five years. Then she tried to get them into an Episcopalian home; Aunt Margaret paid her membership regularly, but I never knew that she attended services. But her parents balked, refused to cooperate, insisted they could keep the apartment they'd lived in ever since my uncle retired from U.S. Steel. Then Phyllis took over.

She saw to it that Aunt Margaret was thoroughly diagnosed. That's when they learned of her embolism; they say almost any little particle of bone or gristle can cause it. She shopped for a nursing home convenient to Jean's home in Waukegan. She persuaded my uncle to live with his daughter and her family. She straightened out his finances. She did everything. Now all there was to do was see that my aunt was comfortable and wait for her to die. Two hours or ten years, there's no telling with an embolism.

We went up the walk to the nursing home with my uncle between us. It had no sign in front; at least it didn't *look* like a nursing home, Phyllis said. "They take good care of her, boy," my uncle said. It had been a long time since anyone called me boy—not since I was in the army perhaps—and hearing it made me feel ignorant and helpless again.

"It's a nice-looking place, Phyllis," I said.

"It's close to Jean's and it's reasonable compared to what they charge some places," she said. "Now don't be surprised when you see her. She's lost so much weight she looks like one of the starving Chinese."

"No good," Uncle Paul said. Years ago his voice had been clear, exact, his pronunciation tinged with a Tennessee accent. Now he croaked and rasped, stopped to swallow often in the middle of a sentence, as if he had to get set to drag up the words from his mind before speaking.

I'm sure it was a very nice nursing home. It wasn't at all like a hospital. The woman Phyllis spoke to at the receptionist's desk wore no starched uniform. There were three old people sitting in the lobby, not dressed in nightgowns or bathrobes, completely normal except for one woman who continually ran a thin scarf through the fingers of one hand. The halls were not lit with fluorescent tubes, and doors were not ajar just enough for someone passing in the corridor to get a peek at a patient's sad, blank face. In an alcove flooded with sunlight, just before we reached my aunt's room, I saw an old man with a stern face reading a book in an old-fashioned, wicker-backed wheelchair.

Aunt Margaret had her eyes closed when we entered, but she wasn't asleep. In the house doctor's report he'd said she hardly ever slept because she was so afraid. Her lunch tray, untouched, lay on the bedside table. She opened her eyes the moment we stopped next to her bed. "I can't eat the food here," she said. She looked at Phyllis, but it may have been an announcement she'd rehearsed for whoever was first to enter her room. "I tell you I can't eat it," she repeated. She had wasted terribly since I last saw her, like the houses of my childhood that had shrunk since I left them. The starving Chinese. I remembered her as a big woman, moving smooth and large in her kitchen, a gourmet chef expert in Spanish recipes, able to read *Don Quixote de la Mancha* in the original with only occasional references to a dictionary.

"Look who I've brought you for a surprise, Aunt Margaret," Phyllis said; "look who's here. I'm Phyllis. It's Phyllis."

"Who'd you think I thought you were?" my aunt said. "Of course you're Phyllis. Did you hear me just say I can't eat this food?" She didn't seem to notice me or her husband. Phyllis gave me a signal with her eyes to stand back and be quiet for a minute, then sat down on the edge of my aunt's bed. Uncle Paul went over to the bedside table and examined the lunch put out by the nursing home. He bent over it, lifted the aluminum cover on the cube steak to smell it. I tried not to stare at either of them.

"Now what's wrong with the food, dear?" Phyllis asked her. "Is there anything you're not supposed to eat for your diet?"

"I just can't eat it."

"Well, then tell me why so I can go talk to the nurse about it. You tell me what you want to eat and I'll see you get it. Tell me now." Phyllis was very patient, very efficient-looking. She had laid one hand on my aunt's wrist. I know if it'd been me there in the bed, I'd have been comforted. Aunt Margaret looked suspiciously at me and her husband without moving her head. She bit her lower lip before speaking, and I made myself check the view from the window of her room. My uncle picked up a dish of peas from her lunch tray and held them up to his nose, then picked one out between two fingers and popped it into his mouth. His jaws worked as if he were chewing a mouthful of meat.

"The food's poisoned," Aunt Margaret whispered loudly to Phyllis.

"Oh, dear heart," she said.

"I'm telling you it's poisoned. Don't you think I know what they're doing out there?" She looked at the door to the corridor. "I hear them. They talk at night and I hear them planning to poison my food. It's poisoned."

"Dear heart, no one wants to poison you," Phyllis said. Uncle Paul picked up the spoon from the tray and began to eat the dish of peas.

"All right, I'll eat it. Then see," she said, and swung her thin legs over the edge of the bed. She took the spoon roughly from her husband's hand, glared at him, and began to eat. My uncle went to the window and Phyllis and I looked at each other. Phyllis raised her eyebrows and looked at the floor: *That's the way it is, here she is and we have to cope with it, make her as comfortable as we can.* My aunt broke the cube steak into pieces with her fork, ate rapidly, all of it, and when she finished the tapioca pudding dessert, scraped the glass dish with her spoon until there was nothing left. Then she got back into bed and waited for us to speak, or perhaps for the first signs of the poison that would prove our folly.

"How are you, Aunt Margaret?" I said.

"I don't sleep."

"You're looking better though, your face is fuller," Phyllis said.

"You know why I can't sleep," she said to Phyllis; she still didn't know me. Uncle Paul began to look through the dresser that held my aunt's belongings. When he found a photograph he took it to the window to see it in the full light.

"Is there too much noise in the hall at night?" Phyllis asked hopefully.

"You know what it is. If I sleep they'll kill me. There's a man out there. He waits out there every night for me to sleep. I heard them. I've been warned. He'll come in and strangle me if I fall asleep. I *have* to stay awake!" Phyllis sighed, made herself comfortable, listened to it all again.

Somehow she thought it began with the doctor, the specialist, who first examined her at Phyllis' request, and detected the embolism. She was never told of the embolism, but she'd traced her move to the nursing home back to him. The others, the nurses, the house doctor, the dieticians and custodial staff, several other patients, were his dedicated agents. She'd eluded him, she thought, and he'd sent these people after her. Her only escape was to remain awake; then *he*, the strong, terrible man who waited to strangle her the moment she fell asleep, didn't dare to touch her.

"That food didn't have real poison in it," she said. "It had drugs to make me sleep, but I'm too strong for that. I only ate it so he wouldn't," and she looked at her husband. At least she recognized him.

"Oh, dear heart," Phyllis said.

"I have to go to the toilet," Uncle Paul said, and started toward the door.

"Then go and be quiet about it," Aunt Margaret snapped back at him.

"Wait just a minute, Uncle Paul, we'll all be going," Phyllis said. She thought that today my aunt just wouldn't know me.

"Listen, dear, you try to rest and eat your supper when it comes, and please sleep, and we'll come back later with Jean this evening," Phyllis said. She smoothed her skirt and picked up her purse. Aunt Margaret's eyes followed us to the door, as though we might allow someone to slip in as we left.

"Goodbye, Aunt Margaret," I said softly, embarrassed, as if I'd spoken baby talk to a puppy or a kitten.

"Buddy," she said, and I went back to her bed. She caught my hand, touched my hair. "I knew it was you all the time, Buddy, but I had to be sure you weren't one of them, don't you see? I know my Buddy when he comes to see me," and she pulled my face close to kiss me. I tried to smile, not to cry.

"How are you, Aunt Margaret. You're going to get better, aren't you."

"I know my sister's own boy, but I had to be sure, you can see that, Buddy." She patted my shoulder, my cheek, my hand. "They're trying to kill me, Buddy, every night that man waits outside the door to kill me and I don't dare sleep. Help me, Buddy, help me, please help me."

"What can I do? I'll do anything I can. I love you, Aunt Margaret." I was crying and smiling now, hearing Phyllis tell Uncle Paul to go down the corridor and ask a nurse if there was a men's room. My aunt touched my wet face and began to cry herself.

"I can't stay awake any more. Did you love your mother, Buddy? If she was alive she'd ask you to help me. Stay here and watch so they don't come in while I sleep. I have to sleep. Do it for your mother if you won't do it for me. Don't you love your aunt? Don't you love your mother's sister? I took care of you when you were small, do you remember that?"

"Phyllis," I said, "tell me something to do, Phyllis. I don't know what to do."

"We have to go, dear heart, we'll be back," she said.

"Oh, won't you help me, Buddy? I'll die. I'll fall asleep and that man will kill me. Help me. Help me, Buddy." Phyllis gave me her handkerchief and I pulled my hands free from my aunt's grasp long enough to wipe my eyes and blow my nose. She leaned forward in the bed, her mouth open as though I could somehow stop the process of an embolism, as if I could command death to halt. "Phyllis is strong, your sister's strong, but she won't help me. She makes me stay here."

To do what I did was almost to believe, for a moment, that I could. And she believed I had.

"Here," I said. I took her hand, opened the clenched fingers, and lifted her palm. I kissed her palm gently and closed her fingers back

over it again. "Now you take that and hold it tight and don't let it get
away. You hold onto that all day until it's time to go to sleep. Then
you put it under your pillow and you go to sleep, because that's a
charm. As long as that's under your pillow nobody can hurt you. Nobody can come into your room and hurt you. Keep it and you'll be
safe." I got up from the bed. Aunt Margaret held her closed hand
against her chest.

"Oh, thank you, thank you, Buddy, you're strong. I knew you
loved me. I knew my dear sister's boy would help me. Thank you,"
and she kept on talking after she closed her eyes and leaned back
against her pillow again. Phyllis had another handkerchief for me
when we were outside in the corridor. I had to help her hunt up my
uncle. Smiling still, to forget I'd cried, I spoke to a lovely old lady
who stood near the floor nurse's station.

"Did you by any chance see an older man wearing a red sweater
come by here a minute ago?"

"You're a horrid ugly dirty nasty man," she spat at me.

"Excuse me." I went back to my sister, who heard.

"Its nice to know it can happen to other people too," she said.

"No, it's not," I said. My uncle came toward us, asking what was
keeping us; he was hungry and wanted to get back to his daughter's
house. "You didn't even speak to her," I said to him.

"It just isn't any good any more, boy, it's no good," he said.

My aunt lived less than a month after that. Phyllis was at her bedside, holding her hand, when she died. She arranged the funeral,
took care of the insurance, selected a plot in the Masonic section of a
cemetery in Waukegan. I was back in New York by then. It's just as
well I couldn't be there then; I wouldn't have known what to do.

My sister Phyllis took care of everythng. She's a tower of strength.